Just Like Elizabeth Taylor

Other Books by Lu Ann Brobst Staheli

Gateway Romance
Temporary Bridesmaid

Small Town U.S.A.
Leona & Me, Helen Marie
A Note Worth Taking

The Explorers
Tides Across the Sea

Timeless Romance Anthology
Silver Bells Collection: "A Fezziwig Christmas"

Non-Fiction
Psychic Madman
Men of Destiny: Abraham Lincoln and the Prophet Joseph
Smith
When Hearts Conjoin: The True Story of Utah's Conjoined
Twins
One Day at a Time: Teaching Secondary English Language
Arts
Books, Books and More Books: A Parent and Teacher's
Guide to Adolescent Literature

Just Like Elizabeth Taylor

Back Yard Press

Lu Ann Brobst Staheli

Cover design by Laura J. Miller
www.anauthorsart.com
Interior Design by Heather Justesen

Editing by Annette Lyon, Heather B. Moore, Michele Paige Homes, Sherri Schloss, and Stephanni Hicken Meyer.

Published by Back Yard Press
ISBN-13: 978-0692316504
ISBN-10: 0692316507

To my sons, Carl, Tommy, Chan, Kent, and Zach, who are survivors of their own stories.

1

I was named after a movie star. Elizabeth Taylor. When Mom was pregnant she watched *National Velvet* on a cable station playing old movies.

"She was so beautiful, and with our last name being Taylor, I couldn't resist," Mom told me. "The doctor in the delivery room placed the tiny bundle that was you across my stomach. Your eyes almost looked violet, and you had a head full of dark hair and a little birthmark on your cheek, just like Elizabeth Taylor. I knew that had to be your name."

"*Liz*, if you please," I reminded her for the millionth time.

I'd read some of the biographies. I didn't want to spoil Mom's impression by telling her that baby Elizabeth Taylor had been ugly, her little newborn body covered all over by dark hair. Mom didn't have any idea that my life—and hers—would turn out to be filled with those same unglamorous experiences her idol had faced. Life wasn't all movie stars and parties like Mom imagined.

After my happy toddler days had passed, I started school unaware that a storm was brewing in my parent's marriage. I wondered why Dad was gone so often, but Mom always said he was on a work trip. The day before he left each time, their voices were louder. By the time I was in third grade, he was coming and going so often I felt like I lived in a bed and breakfast.

Two weeks before Christmas my fifth grade year, I asked Mom, "Is Dad gonna make it home for my holiday concert?" I stood at the wall calendar and counted the days he'd been gone. "How long was his last trip?" I knew exactly how long it had been—fifteen days, with only six before he left again.

"I can't quite remember," Mom said, as she dumped the bowl of bread dough onto the floured counter. She punched the sticky wad, turned it over and punched again.

"He's gonna be home for Christmas, isn't he?" I asked, aware of the sudden panic that made my voice sound funny.

"Hard to say, honey," Mom had answered. "Hard to say."

He pulled into the driveway at nine-thirty-two on Christmas Eve. Three minutes later the yelling started. I heard a door slam and the car engine rev. I didn't think even Macy's Santa could conjure a happy ending out of that one. It was after midnight when I heard the car pull into the driveway. I knew it wasn't Santa in his sleigh.

On Christmas Day the inside of the house was frostier than a snowman. The day after, Dad surprised us both when he said, "Paramount Theater is showing *The Taming of the Shrew* with Elizabeth Taylor. Want to go, Kate?"

Mom had seen it a dozen times. I was too young to

understand Shakespeare. But the three of us going out together sounded like so much fun, I begged to go along. Dad held my hand as we stood in the ticket line. We shared a bucket of buttered popcorn and a soda. We talked about funny memories, and I laughed. No worries today. Mom didn't say ten words the whole time.

When the movie was over and we were pulling out of the parking lot, Dad said, "Ah, Kate, and 'therefore here I mean to take my leave.'"

I recognized the line from the movie and laughed. Ha, ha. But the look on his face told me he wasn't kidding. He was leaving for good. We drove the rest of the way home in silence.

Dad pulled the car into the driveway, and Mom threw open the door. She mumbled something like, "Going to woo Bianca?" She slammed the car door as she ran for the house.

The next day, when he moved out, I chased his car like an unleashed puppy. He didn't stop. Mom ran after me. When she reached me nearly four blocks from the house, she folded me into her arms in the middle of the road. She smoothed the loose strands of hair on top of my head and made lullaby sounds. She was much stronger then. I was the one who couldn't hold my emotions in check.

"Why?" I whispered, and then yelled the same question in the direction his car had gone.

He never answered. Neither did Mom. Instead, she

guided me onto the sidewalk. I shook off the arm she had across my shoulder, and marched away. I cried—no, I screamed, for three hours solid. My throat was so raw that Mom had to take me to the doctor.

"It's better that she gets this rage out," he said.

"Maybe," Mom said. "But the neighbors will think I'm killing her."

"It's Daddy who's killing me," I said, my scratchy voice not even a whisper.

The doctor wrote a prescription for a nasty-tasting liquid that Mom forced me to swallow four times a day until the bottle was empty. It had soothed my throat, but not the pain in my heart.

"When will Dad come home?" I asked over and again.

"He's not," she said every time. Finally I quit asking, there hadn't been any payoff in too long, and we learned in science that even Pavlov's dogs eventually stopped pressing that food bar if they didn't find a treat in the bottom of the cup.

My cup was empty, and I needed to fill it with something else, something that could help me feel better. I discovered the library and started reading everything I could get my hands on. My teacher called me a *voracious* reader. I liked that word.

"You just gulp books down and swallow them whole, Liz," she said.

She was right. I joined the summer reading program at

the public library. I started at the *A*s—Abbott, Adams, Andrews—and worked my way through each shelf, checking out the limit every couple days. I won the Most-Books-Read contest hands down.

Once summer was gone and school started, I didn't stop. I read the entire junior library collection then moved into the adult reading room, hitting the bestsellers table right off the bat. You name it, I read it. The librarian slipped me classics. I got hooked on Dickens. He sure knew how to tell a tale of woe—orphans, pickpockets, convicts, and penny-pinching misers filled his stories. I felt right at home with their sadness.

Three years later, by junior high, I had finally given up hope that Dad would ever pull into the drive. Mom thought she was in love again, so Mark Rogers and his son Ryan moved in six months ago. Because of them, I now live a story that would make Elizabeth Taylor shake her head in empathy, and one Dickens wouldn't dare touch. Mom hadn't seen the bruises I kept hidden. I couldn't tell her. It would hurt her too much to know. I'd gotten over losing my dad, but the pain was back.

2

Mom didn't see the punch coming.

Mark's hand jerked from the potato chip bag and connected with her right cheek quicker than anything. Her head snapped back, and the air escaped from her lungs in a whoosh. I felt like I'd been gut-punched.

"Stay outta my way. I can't see the television," Mark said, his words clipped and angry.

Mom looked stunned next to him on the couch. Tears popped into her eyes, but she winced to hold them back. Mark didn't like tears. She lifted her hand halfway to her face, her mouth working, an imitation of a fish. My heart was pounding like crazy. The room felt hot.

I started to get up from my seat, but sank back down. I looked around for a something to hit him with, something heavy enough to cause damage. Nothing.

I grabbed Mom's Elizabeth Taylor collector doll from the end table. I was twelve now, still flat-chested and skinny as a boy, not strong enough punch to Mark.

A paperback novel I had been reading was on the coffee table in front of me. Useless. I needed something heavy like *The Complete Works of Shakespeare*. Maybe if I could reach Dad—but neither Mom nor I knew where he was.

"Mark," Mom said, but it came out sort of mushed

Lu Ann Brobst Staheli

because she held her hand against the already forming bruise.

"Shut up, woman," Mark said.

My heart jumped into my throat. I worked to steady my breathing, practicing the calming techniques I'd seen on Oprah.

Focus. Focus.

Mark belched. I could smell the sour odor. Three empty cans, crunched by his fist, lay on the scattered newspaper at his feet. *The Times-Tribune.* My gaze narrowed to the front page. Nothing but prom queen photos. Mom had told me she'd once been a prom queen. One look at her face now and no one would believe it.

Mark started to channel-surf his way through the cable sports stations. He'd lost interest in punching people for the moment. My shaking stopped, but the doll was still clenched between my fingers.

"Get me a beer." He didn't even look at her.

I glared at him. I hated Mark, and his stupid son, Ryan.

Mom hesitated a half-second then moved toward the kitchen. Almost before I could blink, she was back, a cold Miller pop-top in her hand. Mark grabbed it without thanking her and guzzled another can, his fourth in less than an hour.

Mom stayed more than an arm's length away from him. She just stood there, her eyes wide like an animal caught by the lights. She gathered the hem of her T-shirt

7

and worked it into her fist, wadding the words *Alexandria, Indiana. Not on the Nile, but Twice as Worthwhile.*

I felt glued to the vinyl recliner. My right fist scrunched the satin fabric of Elizabeth's wedding dress. The doll looked cold, like ice with her alabaster skin and white lace. I had on jeans and a sweatshirt, but still felt chilled. Goose bumps covered my arms beneath the fabric. Rage burned in my heart.

Why couldn't I protect her? Why did Mom just keep standing there? Dad had yelled at her when they fought. He'd never hit her. All those millions of words I had taken in and still nothing to spit out when I needed them.

My head turned away from Mom and Mark. The stations flipped past on the television screen, but I didn't see them. Instead, I saw the punch—instant replay, slow motion, camera zoom, over and over like the airplanes hitting the World Trade Center on CNN. It made me sick.

I wanted to hit Mark, to yell, "Get out of our house!" Instead, I kept fingering the doll's tulle veil and took deep breaths, hoping to think of something to help Mom. Or me.

Mark crunched the emptied can and tossed it to the floor with the others. Before he could speak, Mom slipped into the kitchen and brought the last two cans from the six pack. She set them on the coffee table, backing away then heading again into the kitchen without a glance my direction. We didn't talk much anymore. We never laughed.

8

Pots and pans clattered in the kitchen. Unbelievable! Mom was fixing dinner for that slime. Mark was watching the Indy time-trials report on ESPN. The roaring engines drowned out the low growl I allowed to escape from my throat.

I still missed Dad, missed his laugh. Just yelling at each other didn't seem so bad anymore. Mom used to miss Dad, too.

Then Mark came. She laughed with him for awhile; they seemed to be in love. Not anymore. When was the last time she didn't have that scared-rabbit look on her face? I couldn't remember.

The flame inside me had turned to smoldering embers, but the fire would not die. I hated Mark. And Ryan. And maybe even Mom right now for not standing up for herself.

I needed an escape, a lifeline. I picked up my book, tucked Elizabeth under my arm, and retreated to my room, glad Ryan wasn't home yet.

3

The next day, Mom kept a good distance between herself and Mark's hand. I didn't blame her. I steered clear of Ryan every time he came into the same room.

Mom and I were in the laundry room, folding sheets. The smell of line-dried clothes reminded me that summer had arrived. Mark was at work. I didn't know where Ryan was. Didn't care, as long as it wasn't here at the house.

I looked at Mom's face. I couldn't remember the last time I had seen her smile. The wrinkles around her eyes were new. She was still young, thirty-five. In the past twenty-four hours she had aged.

I had too. I could feel the *old* right to the very middle of my guts. It was hard enough keeping my own secrets, now I'd have to worry about Mom's. Would Mark hit her again?

"Homework tonight?" Her voice matched the lines on her face.

"School ended last Friday," I said, snapping the fabric straight before pulling it up for the final fold. Mom held the other end then walked closer to me, matching the edges to complete the square. It wasn't easy to work in the cramped room.

"Oh, that's right," she said. I was pretty sure she hadn't remembered. Her eyebrows scrunched close like they do when she's trying to put together the answer to a crossword puzzle.

"Mom, why did you let Mark hit you?"

I watched her face crumple. She looked at me a minute before speaking, her voice a fake brightness. "Elizabeth Taylor stayed married to Nicky Hilton even though he hit her."

Mom often quoted the life of Elizabeth Taylor as if it were a manual for her own. The ultimate fan, Mom had read every word ever published, I bet, and she had seen all of Elizabeth's movies over and over.

"They only stayed married a few months, Mom," I said, protest in my voice. "But, you're not married to Mark. Why don't you just tell him to leave?" If she'd asked me the same kind of question, would I have an answer? I wanted to tell her about Ryan, but I couldn't.

"Just like your father?" Mom said.

The question came from left-field. Had Dad left because Mom told him to? She could read my mind I guess, because she answered.

"Yes. I told your father to leave. He was having an affair with his secretary. So cliché, but true." Mom wiped the corner of her eye.

I hadn't seen a tear there. Did she still miss him? Was she wishing Dad was back and Mark gone? I thought I was the only one who felt that way.

She stopped folding clothes and had a far-off look in

her eyes. "She was younger than me, and, I guess, a whole lot prettier. I couldn't think of comparing myself."

Mom was pretty, at least when Dad was with us. Her dark hair framed her heart-shaped face. The sadness in her eyes and pulled-back hair made her look much different now.

"Oh, Mom," I said, stepping forward to put my arms around her neck. I nuzzled into her Mickey Mouse sweatshirt. I loved her, but I had just discovered there was so much about her I didn't understand. Our bodies rocked from side to side as I smoothed her hair, the way she had mine when Dad left. I knew I'd hear another story about Elizabeth Taylor once the moment passed. I wouldn't ever tell her that Nicky Hilton called her idol an 'F—ing bore.' I'd never say that word, but I felt the same way at times when Mom started in with the Elizabeth-tales. Elizabeth-this, and Elizabeth-that. She pulled away after a few seconds.

I couldn't make words come from my mouth to tell her, but I heard them in my head. *Mom, I have an Elizabeth-tale for you, and it's about your daughter this time. And that word—effing—is the very one I need to describe it. Oh, Mom.*

Mom didn't know what Ryan was doing to me. She had all she could manage with his father. If she couldn't escape Mark, how could I ever escape Ryan? Impossible.

I knew to keep my mouth shut, just like she did.

12

Elizabeth didn't get what she expected from Nicky Hilton. No organdy apron and a cottage for Mom either. Too June Cleaver.

And for me? No white dress at my wedding.

I volunteered to take the baskets of folded clothes upstairs and put them away, except for Ryan's, which I left in the hallway outside of his door. I only entered that room when he wouldn't let me escape.

4

On race day, Mark hit Mom again. This time he left a bruise—a real shiner. She called in sick for work, claiming she had a touch of stomach flu. The bruise hadn't faded when he hit her a third time. Mom looked like a prize fighter, black eyes, swollen cheeks. She had to miss more sick days than she had.

When she'd used all her vacation days as well, she was fired from her job. She stayed at home and didn't return phone calls from friends. Soon they stopped calling. I tried to spend every minute of my time at her side. At least I would have some protection, even if she didn't, since Ryan avoided me when the adults were around. Mark hit her whether I was in the room or not.

She didn't fight back. I was afraid to.

I'm not sure exactly when the idea formed, but deep in my heart, I knew I'd leave.

"Elizabeth Taylor never ran away from the bad times. She tried to work them out," Mom said when Dad left.

Maybe Elizabeth should have, I thought. I didn't see any other way. I burrowed into the back of my closet and came up with a Powerpuff Girls backpack I had abandoned two years ago, at the end of sixth grade. Mom hadn't done much cleaning since Mark came. I dumped the old school papers into the trash can. The pack wasn't very big, but I didn't own a suitcase so it would have to do.

I started to collect things I would need. Granola bars, soap, the Barney toothbrush from the dentist that I had never opened a roll of toilet paper just in case, and a metal can opener.

"Liz, have you seen the hand-crank can opener anywhere?" Mom asked me a week after I had stolen it from the back of the drawer where it had hidden for months.

"No, Mom." I felt like a thief.

I packed and re-packed my clothes. An extra pair of jeans, four T-shirts, a sweatshirt, half dozen pair of socks, six panties, and a bra Mom had just picked up at Kmart. If I tried to squeeze anything else into the bag, the seams would pop. I'd have to buy stuff along the way. But with what?

Twenty-six bucks. Summer was over, and that's all I had saved. It wouldn't be enough to live a week on, let alone forever. Forever? I hoped not.

I added school and medical records to the outside pocket of my stash. I liked school and might be able to enroll. I'd seen a Saturday morning sitcom about a girl checking into a new school. She didn't have the right papers so they wouldn't let her. It made sense to me. Good thing Mom still remembered to file copies. Correction fluid altered the name, and a photocopy looked like an original.

Mom had spent days covered in bruises. She wasn't going to get rid of Mark. Could I stand being touched by Ryan one more time? I didn't think so. There had to be a quicker way to save money. Money meant *escape*.

Just Like Elizabeth Taylor

I was mulling my options as I entertained the two neighbor girls I sometimes babysat. They stood on their side of the narrow street; I on mine. No other neighbors were outside. The late August afternoon sun beat against the driveway. I squatted to slide Mom's Elizabeth Taylor doll into the pink Corvette the girls and I had been passing back and forth. I'd latched onto that doll. Somehow it gave me comfort. I thrust the car forward, letting it speed from my hand toward the girls.

"Escape, Elizabeth. Escape," I whispered.

The girls squealed. They held their hands against their faces as runaway Elizabeth scooted through the path of a pick-up truck driving too fast. The back tire crushed the plastic, leaving Corvette-pancake and beaten-Elizabeth before the truck turned into our drive. Ryan slammed on the brakes and shut off the engine.

"What's he doing home?" one of the girls asked when she saw him climb down.

"Don't know," I said. My heart raced. Football practice must have ended early. "Go on home now, girls." They scooted around the side of their house. I wanted to go, too.

Ryan grabbed my wrist. He worked out with weights and was strong. I pulled, but he held on tight. As always, fighting him was useless. I opened my mouth to scream, but no sound came out.

"Get in the house now." His hot breath was close against my ear. "You know you can't escape. I always get it."

16

I tried to kick him, but he gave me a shove with his free hand. I stumbled toward the screened porch. His grip didn't loosen as he jerked my arm, pulling me closer on our way inside.

The interior of the clapboard house felt baked, but my body was cold from hatred. I shivered. I knew what was coming next. He pushed me up the staircase ahead of him, his free hand exploring my waist where he had yanked my shirt loose from my waistband. I stumbled, but he held fast, still gripping my wrist with his other hand. My joints nearly ripped with the force he used to jerk me to my feet.

"Keep moving." His voice was a growl, low in his throat.

We were alone in the house. He always made sure. He pushed me, letting go of my hand. I crashed into the bed frame and slumped to the floor, then heard the click of the lock. The curtains were closed. He liked the room dark.

I buried my head into the covers, hoping he would change his mind. But knowing he never did. He tugged my head back with my braid.

"Come on, Lizzy." His voice was muted, a failed attempt to be seductive like the R-rated videos he watched in our living room. "Don't you want some lovin'?"

Loving? Ryan didn't even *like* me.

He placed his hands under my arms and lifted me onto the bed. I beat my hands against his sides. It made no difference. He towered over me as he unbuttoned my

17

blouse. I tried to wrap my arms to cover my nakedness, but he had something else in mind. My skin became numb against his weight, and I took quick little gasps of air through my mouth. Maybe I'd hyperventilate. I jabbed my knee near his groin. I wanted to kill him before passing out.

"Get off me," I said. The words escaped through gritted teeth. I scraped my fingernails deep against his chest.

His slobbery tongue dipped into my ear. His weight shifted lower onto my pelvis. I was trapped.

A few minutes later, he was gone. I picked up my clothing he had strewn around the room and scurried to the door. Ryan's truck motor ground into gear and the tires squealed as he left the driveway. No other sounds from the house below. Alone.

"I can't take anymore," I yelled into the silence. Couldn't I find a way to earn money once I was gone?

I slipped from Ryan's room and padded down the hallway to my own, locking the door behind me. Dropping the clothes into the hamper beside my closet door, I gathered fresh underwear, a pair of sweats, and an oversized towel, before rushing to the bathroom for a shower, the water turned as hot as my raw skin could stand it. I stood in the blasting spray, screaming like I had the day Dad left. Tears coursed my cheeks, mixing with the water until it turned cold.

At last I turned off the faucet.

When I had dressed and gone downstairs in search of something to eat, I found Mark. I hadn't heard anyone come home because of the pelting water. His snoring breath stunk of bourbon as he sprawled, passed out, on the living room couch. He'd stopped at the bar. Mom would be a target tonight. Her last bruises had faded. It still made me sick to see him hit her, but I couldn't save her unless I somehow saved myself.

I went into the kitchen to make a sandwich. A wad of cash sat on the table. I grabbed it and counted the bills. Over three hundred dollars. His paycheck. I couldn't believe my luck. What would he do to me if the money was gone? What would he do to Mom? How much worse could it possibly be?

I had no other choice but to run.

My decision made, I went to my room and picked up the backpack. Now was the time.

5

I could see the "Welcome to Anderson" sign long before I reached it. The big black letters stenciled onto a white, scrolled plywood that were nailed to short poles plugged deep into the ground like telephone poles.

Welcome. It called out to me. I hadn't really planned to stop here, but the nine mile bike ride had already taken over an hour, and the backpack straps were wearing blisters on my arms. I should have changed into a top with sleeves before I started. Too late now.

I was worried someone might find me and I'd have to go home. If home meant just my mother, I would have gone in a second, but I could not, would not, return to her if Mark and Ryan were still there.

I figured I could stay overnight here and get a fresh start in the morning. Final destination, unknown. But that darn old sign seemed to be calling to me. *Welcome. Welcome.* Each pedal closer brought the word more clearly into focus and lodged it more deeply into my brain. My thoughts were racing around like the cars at the Indy 500. I hoped I had run far enough.

Anderson was a familiar place. Bigger than Alexandria, three high schools here and only one back home. But Anderson still felt like small town, Hoosier hospitality and all that. I'd been here a few times when Dad was still at home with us. He'd brought me down to the Kmart. Alexandria doesn't have one, and Dad liked to browse the aisles just in case he saw something he couldn't live without, even though he'd just discovered his need while standing in the aisle.

Anderson had another good thing going for it. I saw a familiar sign attached to the speed limit sign, warning drivers to slow down before they hit the city limits. I remembered a family camping vacation, when we were still a family. Dad borrowed a pop-up trailer from someone at work. Mom packed clothing and brought food. We drove until we pulled up to a parking lot for trailers and campers. The sign overhead said, "Welcome to K.O.A."

"What's koa?" I asked.

Mom and Dad both laughed and Dad told me it wasn't *koa*, but K.O.A. "It stands for Kampgrounds of America."

I was in second grade, but I was sure *campgrounds* started with a *C* and not a *K*. I didn't say anything. I didn't want to start an argument. Mom and Dad had enough of them on their own without help from me.

All that seemed so long ago now. But I still remembered the running water in the showers and the toilets. I remembered the electric plugs by the cement pads. I remembered the campground was close enough to town that Mom was able to walk for a six pack of sodas when we ran out.

I stopped at the first convenience store I saw once I hit

town and used the phone book to locate the K.O. A. Following the map I ripped from the yellow pages, I didn't have any trouble finding the site. It wasn't far from where I had stolen the map.

No cars were in the lot, and none had passed me for the last several blocks as I rode my bike. I skirted the crossed logs at the gate and scoured the length of the park, two rows of parking slots in the main driveway. Several branching drives went into the trees, and I checked out each one, finding nothing to indicate people had been here for at least a few weeks.

In a spur that went into the wooded area, I noticed someone had left a beat-up mattress and ratty blanket. There was a storage shed just behind where the mattress was. I'd stumbled onto a goldmine. The area was away from the main drive and would be perfect for me to set up camp.

Luck was with me. The door swung open, and the shed was empty. I noticed two electric plug outlets near the baseboard. The place seemed as good as any to set up residence. I figured I could make it through until spring, somehow, with a place to sleep and money in my pocket. No one would be the wiser. There didn't seem to be an office on the grounds, so I doubted anyone checked the area during the winter months. Labor Day was a few days away yet, but it looked like this campground was already closed for the season.

I found a sturdy stick and beat some of the pent-up dust from the mattress. I sniffed. It didn't smell too bad for having been left outside. I pulled it into the shed and slid it against the back wall. Next, I shook the blanket out. It was cotton cloth, so I took it over to the nearby tourist facilities—the toilet and showers—and rinsed it, wishing I had soap. I hung the blanket over a low tree branch to dry while I surveyed the rest of the campgrounds a second time.

Not much else had been left. A few broken toys, a single glove, and a smashed McDonald's cup. I picked up the glove and tossed it onto the mattress. The toys went into the empty trash bin a few stalls from mine. The stale smell of garbage didn't drift far. I smoothed out the crinkled cup as much as I could, picked a sprig of mums from the plant near the campground's entrance, and placed it by the mattress. I dug Elizabeth Taylor from my backpack, where I had tossed her, and sat her up in the middle of the mattress.

Food was not an immediate problem. I still had a can of pork and beans stuffed into my backpack, taken from the pantry. I'd been on the road for less than a day, but, so far, I was doing okay. Now I had a place to live, and lots of time to think.

The idea came to me to enroll in school. School seemed so ordinary. Normal. A safe place. Who would think to look for a run-away in a school? I hoped no one but me. I was glad I'd packed the paperwork I would need.

I enjoyed school, even when my former teachers asked me about the bruises Ryan gave me. "Bumped into the door jam last night," or "I'm so clumsy, always slamming my legs and arms into stuff without paying any attention. I'm fine." I had gotten good at lying.

School would give me a place to blend in. A place to learn. A place to get a hot meal at least once a day, as long as I had money. Sometimes I might stop in for breakfast. I didn't want people to notice I didn't have a mom to fix breakfast. I didn't want to think about that too much myself.

The first day was lonely, hiding from traffic wherever I could as I rode farther and farther away from home, setting up the shed to be a home for me. But the night was worse. I cried myself to sleep, thinking about Mom.

***

The next morning, I sat in a wooden chair next to the guidance secretary's desk. Mrs. Elder, her nameplate read. Couldn't have been more appropriate, I thought. She looked like she was old enough to be someone's great-grandmother, gray-haired, stooped shoulders, and flappy skin drooping all over her face. She asked the questions. I gave the answers.

Elizabeth—Liz—Taylor. Wrong.

"Elizabeth—Beth—Burton." I had chosen the last name because of Elizabeth Taylor's true love—Richard Burton. Beth was a nickname for Elizabeth, although a little outdated, but I didn't care. I figured it would make it easier to remember a new name if it was like my old one.

"218 West Millard Avenue." *The K.O.A. Campgrounds.*

"Parents: Bob and Jessie Burton." *Bogus names for my non-family.*

The ancient counselor typed the information into the computer. She probably would have been more comfortable using an old IMB Selectra instead of the computer screen flashing before her.

"My parents are both starting new jobs and couldn't come to register me."

"Happens all the time," Mrs. Elder said. "Phone number?"

"It's not hooked up yet. We just moved in."

She peered at me a second before asking, "Cell phone?"

Crap! I hadn't thought about that. I shrugged my shoulders. "I don't have their numbers memorized."

"Bring them as soon as you can," she said. "Do you have your immunization records?"

Those I did have, thanks to the TV show I'd watched. "Yes, ma'am." She looked them over briefly, made a photocopy for her records then handed the pages back to me.

"Everything seems in order," she said. "Requirements: English, Math, Science, History, Gym. Elective?"

"What's that?" I was new to middle school, so I didn't

know all the classes yet. Elective was one I'd never heard of.

"You choose." The woman reviewed a chart of course listings in front of her. "Looks like choir is the only thing open the period you need filled."

I couldn't hit a note, let alone stay on the same one for more than a second, but choir it was, even though it wasn't my choice. Mrs. Elder completed the registration form, had me sign the bottom line, and ripped the back card off to put into the inbox on her desk. She handed me the pages, along with a late admit slip.

"Take a right turn out of the office and go four classrooms on the left. You'll still make first period," she said.

"Thanks," I said before moving into the empty hall. I found the classroom easily enough. The nameplate next to the teacher's photo said Mrs. Latham. I entered and thrust the admit slip and registration card toward her. She took it and read my name.

"Elizabeth Burton?" Mrs. Latham looked from the admit slip into my eyes. I glanced toward the floor.

"Beth." The name felt odd coming from my mouth.

She pulled her bifocals down an inch on her thin nose and looked me over. *Is every adult in this school going to be this old?* I felt the dampness of my palms. I didn't want to be standing at the front of the classroom filled with strangers. I wanted to sink into a seat as the newest student at Highland High.

"Are you related to the Burton family on Sycamore Street?"

"I don't think so." I wasn't related to anyone named Burton, but I couldn't let her know that. Lying was not going to be quite as easy as I thought it would be.

"You look a bit like their daughter, Marie," Mrs. Latham said. "But, since you're from out of state, probably not. Have a seat in the back of the second row."

"Thank you," I said. I situated myself, trying to blend in. No such luck. The red-headed girl in the seat in front of mine immediately twisted around to get a better look.

"Hi. My name's Ida Mae Ruth. And you're Beth Burton."

She had freckles across the bridge of her nose and her teeth were too large to fit inside her mouth, which was opened wide in a grin. I could tell Ida Mae Ruth was waiting for me to launch right into a full-blown conversation, something I was not going to do. Nothing against her. She seemed a nice enough girl.

"That's right," I said and tried to appear busy, pulling my notebook and a pencil from the beat-up book bag I found in the school dumpster late last night. I spent a quarter this morning at a corner convenience store for the notebook, and I picked up the pencil in the hallway before I entered the counselor's office. You could always count on the hallway for a pencil.

I wanted to fit the role of a new student and not draw

attention to myself. I wanted a chance to start over, away from Ryan. I'd work out getting back with Mom later. I didn't want to answer questions, even from fellow students. I knew there were too many holes in my story, and I wanted to work them out at my own rate. Ida Mae didn't notice my reluctance.

"When did you move in? I've lived here all my life. Do you have any brothers or sisters? I don't right now. What's your favorite movie? I like romances. Ever been to a hockey game?"

I continued to stare through her, trying to listen beyond her chatter to Mrs. Latham at the front of the room. She looked toward us, stopping her lecture on drama.

"Miss Ruth."

I bolted straight up in my chair at the tone Mrs. Latham used, but Ida Mae continued to prattle.

"Don't you ever talk? What sort of music do you listen to? I live near West Millard Avenue. We'll ride the same bus to school."

I focused on what Ida Mae was saying to me.

"Do you think we can be friends?"

"No!" I said. I was startled by the forcefulness of my own voice. I didn't want to sound angry or mean, but I couldn't allow anyone to find out my truth.

"Miss Ruth." Mrs. Latham stood at Ida Mae's desk. I had not seen the teacher move near us.

"You don't?" Ida Mae asked again, her voice rising

like she either didn't believe me, or she was trying not to cry.

"No," I said.

Ida Mae's face fell; her lip quivered. She turned around in her seat.

"Miss Ruth, I hope your conversation is finished," Mrs. Latham said, tapping her finger against the top of Ida Mae's desk.

"Yes, Mrs. Latham," Ida Mae said, her voice suddenly more unsure if itself.

I didn't see Ida Mae Ruth the rest of the day. I would be fine if could keep it that way.

***

I rode my bike to and from school those first few days after I enrolled. I wasn't anxious to give Ida Mae Ruth another chance to start asking questions. She sat facing the front of the room in Mrs. Latham's class, working hard at proving to me I didn't exist. She needn't have worked so hard.

On my way to school one morning, a morning I'd decided to take a break from pedaling and walk instead, I passed her standing alone at the bus stop. She wasn't really alone. A group of smaller children were playing off to the side of the road, calling out toward her. Their words sounded like a jump rope rhyme.

"Ida Mae. Ida Mae. Hasn't got a friend today. No one in the town will say, 'I want to play with Ida Mae.'"

Then they laughed. Ida Mae stood stock-still and stared down the road, her head held high, pretending she didn't hear. I looked the same direction and saw the school bus, still a little yellow spot, but getting nearer. Why not ride the bus? I thought, staying out of sight in case Ida Mae looked toward me. Ida Mae was a chatterbox to me the first day, but since then I noticed she spoke to no one, and no one spoke to her, with the exception of what I had just heard.

After a few minutes, the bus pulled to a screeching halt not a foot away from Ida Mae's toes. The door creaked open and Ida Mae climbed the steps with heavy feet. The group of children gathered their school books and jackets and piled onto the bus. I noticed a couple of girls our age were among them, but I hadn't learned anyone else's name. I hurried past Ida Mae, finding myself a seat. She took the seat behind the driver and was babbling to her with a list of questions like she threw at me my first day, her voice carrying over the noise of the bus.

"How are you today, Mrs. Stevens? I think I'm getting a cold. Don't you ever get tired of driving this bus? Do the kids drive you crazy? Isn't it a beautiful morning?"

Mrs. Stevens didn't answer Ida Mae's questions, but Ida Mae didn't stop talking. No one seemed to pay any attention to me, either. I was glad. I opened the book I borrowed from the school library and began to read.

Almost before I knew it, we were at school. The bus emptied quickly, so I was the last one out. I didn't mean to be. I rushed past Mrs. Stevens, hoping she hadn't noticed me as someone new.

"See you this afternoon," Mrs. Stevens said as I went down the steps.

"Yeah," I said and headed toward the building, glad I hadn't been recognized as a newcomer, but also wondering why Ida Mae wasn't included more. She seemed like a kid who would be hard to miss.

6

The next few weeks passed quickly. School was going well, and I enjoyed my classes. My teachers seemed to like me, and I was even learning to stay on the right note once in a while in choir.

"Nice job today, Beth," Mrs. Mitchell said to me at the end of class. I still felt warm inside from the praise. I couldn't remember the last time someone said something nice to me. Oh, I suppose I could, but it had been a long time ago it seemed.

I was still humming to myself as I climbed on the bus headed for home. The cooler weather and the fact that Mrs. Stevens hadn't thrown me off for not belonging had helped me abandon my daily bike ride to and from school, carrying a heavy backpack. The bus seemed to be crowded for some reason. It was Friday and I remembered what I had seen and heard in class this morning.

Jill Kimball—a name I had just learned—was having a birthday party this afternoon. I heard her talking about it with the other girls in my English class, except Ida Mae. They huddled around Jill, squealing and chatting about how much fun they would have and what video they would watch and the food they would eat. Ida Mae sat silent, her nose stuck in a book.

I was eavesdropping. It made me sad to think I would

never again be able to have close friends like Jill. I heard a sniffle from the seat in front of me. Ida Mae ran her arm across her eyes, and I noticed the wetness left on her sleeve. She was crying.

I was so wrapped up in my own sadness it took me a minute to realize Ida Mae was just as lonely as I was, listening to the girls talk. I missed the friends I had before Mark came. I missed Mom. Ida Mae didn't seem to have anyone. I assumed she had a mom, but who knew? Ida Mae had been serious when she asked me if we could be best friends. I hadn't meant to hurt her feelings. Not really. But I guess I had.

Then I remembered the rhyme the kids used at the bus stop. Everyone hurt her feelings. Ida Mae was all alone in the world.

Just like me.

Although I understood how she must feel, I knew in my heart I couldn't do anything about it. It would be too easy to leave a trail if Mom was looking for me. I couldn't go back. Not as long as she was living with them. No matter how much I missed Mom and the way she used to be before they came.

Jill and her friends filled the available seats toward the back of the bus. I was forced to sit in the only empty seat, directly across the aisle from Ida Mae, but she didn't notice.

"Good afternoon, Mrs. Stevens. Did you have a good

lunch? How is your husband? Do you think it will rain? What are you doing tomorrow?" Her constant series of questions were left unanswered as Mrs. Stevens drove the bus.

I opened the book I was assigned and began to read. *It was the best of times, it was the worst of times. . .* A perfect book for my miserable weekend, alone.

The bus ride was uneventful. I glanced out once to see Ms. Meyers from the cafeteria snack line at school. She was taking groceries from a car parked in a driveway. She looked about my mom's age, but I couldn't be sure. Ms. Meyer's was tall compared to the other lunch workers and added about three more inches by teasing her hair. Her tan suggested she liked the outdoors, and I assumed she was athletic since she was thin. She always sounded cheerful when she spoke to the kids.

I usually went through the hot lunch line run by old Mrs. Neiderbraun. She wore a sour face and recounted the money, as if she were certain we were trying to cheat her out of a penny. Although I still had cash in my pocket, I'd been offering to do odd jobs for people downtown after school to replace what I spent. I watched money just as carefully as Mrs. Neiderbraun. But, maybe I should check out Ms. Meyer's line someday.

Soon we were at our bus stop, and Ida Mae and I waited while Jill's friends burst through the aisle from behind, all giggly and excited for the party to officially begin. They didn't even acknowledge us as they plowed past our front row seats, out the doorway, and through the group of smaller children, who carried book bags almost as big as themselves. There was an awkward moment as both Ida Mae and I tried to enter the aisle at the same time.

"Sorry," she said as she moved back farther into her seat.

"You first," I said as I stepped back into my seat.

Ida Mae waited. I waited.

Finally, Mrs. Stevens said, "Should I toss a coin to see who goes first?" We both shook our heads. *No.* Ida Mae moved into the aisle. I followed her down the stairs and turned toward the campgrounds. Mrs. Stevens pulled the door handle shut and the engine revved again to life. The bus pulled away from the curb where Ida Mae continued to stand. I could feel her staring at me. I started to walk. With the bus gone, the street was now quiet. Jill's crowd had disappeared into one of the homes across the block.

"See you Monday, Ida Mae," I said before putting my brain into gear. I don't know what possessed me to say it. I didn't turn around but just kept walking toward the shed I called home.

"Sounds great, Beth." Ida Mae's giggle rang out as I heard her feet run up the sidewalk, across the lawn, then the banging of a screen door behind her. Again, silence.

I was alone on the street, but I no longer felt quite so alone.

7

Monday morning our new routine started. Ida Mae stood at the bus stop, as usual. The little kids played on the lawn nearby. I walked toward Ida Mae. She looked at me. I looked at her.

She nodded and said, "Hello."

I nodded and said, "Hi." That was all.

We stood, waiting in silence until the bus came. Ida Mae climbed on first and took her usual seat behind Mrs. Stevens. She started in immediately with her one-sided conversation. I took the seat across the aisle from Ida Mae. I opened my book and continued to read. I'd not quite finished the evening before and thought I could read the last chapter on the way to school. *As the deathcarts rumbled to the guillotine . . .*

Ida Mae continued her incessant chatter while Mrs. Stevens guided the bus on our regular route. Soon a new rumble worked its way toward me from the back of the bus. I finally understood the words.

"Ms. Meyers. It's Ms. Meyers. The lunch lady. Look at her." I glanced back over my left shoulder to see kids starting to stand up and look out the windows on my side of the bus. Some of them had their mouths gawking open. "What's she doing?"

"Ms. Meyers," someone yelled. "Didn't you forget something?"

I looked through the window and saw a tuft of hair standing straight up, teased by the wind. It was Ms. Meyers. We weren't travelling fast since we were in the city limits, moving from one bus stop to the next. I noticed her eyes were glazed as she ran on the sidewalk alongside the bus. The thought flashed through my mind, why is she running? Maybe her car . . .

Then my eyes registered what I was seeing and just about popped out of my head. Ms. Meyers was naked.

"Stop the bus!" I yelled, catching Mrs. Steven's attention and Ida Mae's, too. The bus came to an immediate halt, but Ms. Meyers kept running, not even breaking stride.

"Oh, my God," Mrs. Stevens said as she grabbed the CB microphone. "We have an emergency." She shouted into the handset. Mrs. Stevens must have heard the name and made the connection because she said into the mic, "Ms. Meyers from the school lunchroom is running down the road in front of us, and she's naked." The last word came out in a screech which stuck in my heart like an arrow.

Naked.

I broke into a cold sweat. I remembered my own running, trying to get away from him. Then he caught me. "No!" I shouted. The sound of my voice startled me. I snapped my jaw shut, jammed the marker into my book, and climbed on the seat to frantically search the overhead bin. I knew Mrs. Stevens kept a blanket on the bus. I'd seen her use it on one of the little kids at the end of the day when he didn't feel well.

"Where's the blanket? Where's the blanket?" Even though I had never spoken to Ms. Meyers, I knew something was terribly wrong. "Where's the blanket?"

No answer. Mrs. Stevens was busy talking into the microphone, and the students were all kneeling in their seats, trying to crane their necks out of the bus windows to see where Ms. Meyers had gone.

Ida Mae jumped onto her seat and started searching the overhead bin on her side. "It's not here," she said.

I knew I had to move faster when I heard Mrs. Stevens ask over her radio, "Should I call the police?" and a bevy of responses snapped back from drivers along the route. Everyone knew. All the drivers. All the kids.

I must protect Ms. Meyers. At last my fingertips touched a fragment of the rough blanket, and I jumped to get a better hold. I felt Ida Mae's hands steady me from falling. I reached once more and my fingers found the material from the compartment. I tugged it loose.

"Open the door," I said, as I ran down the steps, the blanket trailing behind me. Mrs. Stevens grabbed the handle, and the doors folded back before me. I started a dead run toward the now distant Ms. Meyers. "Ms. Meyers! Stop, Ms. Meyers!" I yelled as she continued to streak before me. The gravel under my feet caused me to slip and slide in my efforts to catch up.

I heard Ida Mae's voice above all the rest. "Hurry, Beth. Hurry."

"Ms. Meyers!" I yelled once more. "Stop!"

She did. She turned her head toward me and cocked her ear as if listening to a voice calling her from far away. I continued to run, but I, too, picked up a faint sound from the distance. Sirens. The police were coming. I poured every ounce of energy I possessed into reaching Ms. Meyers before the police could.

As I neared her, I held the blanket out in front of me and turned my head toward the side. I slowed my pace and bumped into her before wrapping the blanket around her, trying to cover up all the important parts. She stood still, arms at her sides. Her eyes continued to stare unfocused. I understood her glazed eyes and awareness of nothing. Even though I didn't know what had happened to her, I was sure I had been to the same terrible place. Something horrible must have happened to Ms. Meyers.

The squad car rolled to a halt and a female officer exited from the driver's side. "Good job," she said to me. "We'll handle it from here."

I noticed an ambulance had pulled up behind the police car. People started closing in around Ms. Meyers, and I was pushed out. I stood shivering, filled with the deep down cold I had felt too many times before. There were hands on my shoulders, guiding me toward the bus.

It was Ida Mae. "Everything will be okay," she said to

me as I climbed the steps and reseated myself in the bus. The other kids were all—oddly, with the exception of Jill Kimball—gathered on the side where Ms. Meyers stood with the officer and paramedics. They stared at Ms. Meyers as she stared past the officers. Jill sat huddled in her seat, looking out the opposite set of windows. I hadn't even heard the bus pull up for all the noise the sirens made. By some miracle, or perhaps because their own shock set in, the kids were quiet—even Ida Mae. She returned to her seat, the moment passed between us.

I opened my book to the marked place and began to read, hoping to shut out the painful images as Mrs. Stevens ground the gears into place and the bus jerked away.

"It is a far, far better thing that I do, than I have ever done; it is a far, far better rest that I go to than I have ever known."

8

Once we arrived at school, it didn't take long for word to spread—all of the bus students heard the announcement from the bus intercom system, anyway. There were titters and giggles, jokes and gossip flying from chair to chair and table to table around the classroom. My first period English class was uncontrollable. I felt sorry for Mrs. Latham.

By the end of first period, word spread I was the one who had taken the blanket to cover Ms. Meyers. In the few weeks I had attended the school, no one much spoke to me, other than Ida Mae. I had remained anonymous. Not today. They gathered around me like locust.

"What was wrong with Ms. Meyers?"

"Did she say anything crazy to you?"

"Why'd you take her a blanket?"

What could there possibly be for me to say? I refused them all with my silence, a skill I perfected long ago. By the time lunch rolled around, the crowd gave up on me, although the buzz of chatter was louder than usual. This was, after all, Ms. Meyers' domain and everyone tried to pump information from the other lunch ladies who were more subdued than usual.

I waited my turn in line, not speaking to anyone. Mrs. Neiderbraun smiled, which I returned. I could see students whispering and pointing at me, but I ignored them. I collected my silverware, tray, and milk carton then headed for my usual spot in the far corner of the room. Here I knew I would be alone to think my own thoughts and read a chapter or two of a new book. I sat down and flipped to the first chapter, ready to feast both my mind and my stomach.

"Is this seat taken?" Ida Mae Ruth said.

Startled, I looked up from my book and shook my head. Ida Mae placed her tray on the table, slid into the seat, and opened her own book. She began to read and eat. I sat there a minute, just watching her, but she didn't seem inclined to talk. I was grateful and returned to my reading and meal.

When I was through, the bell rang to return to class.

Ida Mae and I took math together right after lunch, so I wasn't surprised when she picked up her tray and followed me to the dish return slot, then dogged my steps toward the classroom. I slipped into my seat at the same time Ida Mae took hers. Class was nothing unusual, and Mr. Davis was experienced enough to cut the gossip left over from the lunchroom almost immediately.

"You will respect your elders," he said, and the class set to work.

At the end of the period, I was a little startled to realize Ida Mae was again following right behind me as I walked to the gym for sixth period. Ida Mae didn't have gym this period. She waited for me to enter the locker room. When I peeked back into the hall a few minutes later, she was gone.

Basketball. I knew I wouldn't play much. That was okay. I wasn't very good at it. The girls in my gym class were competitive, and I wasn't part of their group. I took my place at the end of the bench to wait for the shower bell to ring.

Once I was dressed at the end of class, I opened the door into the hallway, and there was Ida Mae, waiting for me. She followed me to the room where I had science. She stopped a second, then walked to the next classroom and went in. *Strange*, I thought.

At the end of the day, there she was again. Ida Mae followed me to my locker, rummaged in her own a few units down, then silently followed me to the bus and slipped into her usual seat.

The next day was the same. Ida Mae waited for me at the end of each class, walked behind me to the door, then disappeared to her own class until time to come retrieve me. By the third day, I was trying to lose her, unsuccessfully, at best. By the fourth day, I'd given up. Let her be, I thought as I continued to come and go like I would without Ida Mae as my shadow. No one else seemed to notice her, so why should I care.

9

Other than a "Hello" at the bus stop, Ida Mae and I still weren't talking to each other a week later. Ida Mae continued to follow me everywhere, though. I hadn't decided yet how it made me feel. Was she still hoping to be my friend? Or was she trying to be my protector? The other students occasionally questioned me about the incident when Ida Mae wasn't around. I didn't respond.

Mostly, talk of that morning died to nothing. No one seemed to know what happened to Ms. Meyers after the ambulance took her away. Even the usual sources—kids whose mothers worked at the hospital—didn't know anything. I was glad to move on, and since Ida Mae seemed happy following me around, I learned to accept her silent company. I had other worries on my mind, worries of my own.

Fall settled in for good now and my shed was getting chilly at night. I began to think about how I could provide heat for the place without drawing attention to my living conditions. Also, I was beginning to need warmer clothes. It had been summer when I left home and my few pieces of clothing were geared more toward hot days. I didn't want to spend much money, saving all I could for food. It wasn't always easy to pick up jobs, especially now that people were more inclined to stay indoors from the rain and cool air. Gardening was long past its prime and that, or weeding had been the easiest ways to earn a few dollars.

I'd been filling up at school by eating everything on the hot lunch tray, including foods I normally would have passed by, like carrot *Jell-o*, pickled beets, and mystery meat burritos. I'd even managed to snatch an abandoned apple or two and taken them home to add to my after-school snack supply. I had to be careful not to be seen, though. I didn't want anyone to start asking questions I couldn't answer. That's why I needed to think about new clothes. Once winter set in, I couldn't still be wearing short-sleeved tops without a coat or jacket. People would know something was wrong.

On Saturday, I walked into town and found my way to the mall. It was jam-packed with people of all ages. I even saw a few kids from the middle school, but I didn't speak to them. The teachers were pretty good about letting me just come to class and do my work without questioning me. Unless I had to talk to them, I spent most of my time with my head down, either reading or writing, and I would just smile with a look of innocence when I was spoken to. It didn't take them long to catch on I didn't have much to say, and since I got good grades on all my written work, they didn't press. The high grades also insured the teachers weren't concerned when my parents didn't show up for parent teacher conferences at the end of the first term.

Just a few minutes of browsing through the stores

proved to me new clothes from the mall were out of the question. How did families with lots of kids ever afford to dress them? Jeans started at fifty bucks and a sweatshirt thirty-five. Shoes were outrageous, running upwards from seventy-five. I knew this was getting me nowhere. Just as I started to leave, I heard someone call my name.

"Beth Burton. Beth."

It took me a minute to locate her, but I recognized the voice. It was Ida Mae. She was waving at me from across the food court. Standing at her side was a woman I assumed to be her mother. I waved back and continued toward the exit. Then, I remembered my manners. My mom might have changed a lot after Dad left and Mark came, but I could still hear her reminders to be polite, especially toward adults. I turned back around and said, "Hello, Ida Mae."

That was her signal. Ida Mae rushed across the expanse between us, towing her mother behind her. "Beth, I'd like to introduce you to my mother," she said, a bit out of breath in her excitement.

"So nice to meet you, Mrs. Ruth," I said, putting my hand out to be shaken. I noticed she didn't share Ida Mae's bright red hair or freckles.

"She's the one I told you gave Ms. Meyers the blanket when she was naked," Ida Mae said. Her mother looked at her and gave her head a little shake of disapproval, but the smile remained in place.

"So nice to meet you, Beth. I've heard such nice things about you from Ida."

"Today's my birthday," Ida Mae said.

I was a bit embarrassed. It was obvious Ida Mae had spoken about me to her mother more than I had thought about her. Ida Mae must have considered me a friend, yet I didn't even know when her birthday was. "Hap . . . Happy Birthday," I said.

"Ida Mae," her mother said. "How would you like to invite Beth over to your birthday party and to spend the night?" I saw Ida Mae's face brighten at the offer of the party, but she immediately looked concerned when her mother added the invitation to spend the night.

"Well, I . . ." I said, but Ida Mae jumped right in.

"Would you like to come for my party? It's nothing really special, just Mother and Daddy and me, but there will be cake."

Birthday cake sounded tempting, but I didn't know if I could trust Ida Mae's parents not to question me about my family. "Well, I . . ." I said again.

"I'm sure you'll want to ask your mother for permission to stay over, Beth," Mrs. Ruth said. "Why don't you plan on coming around six for some cake and ice cream? You can let us know then if you'd like to sleep over."

"Well, I . . ." I said once more.

"Will you come?" Ida Mae said. Other than her constant chatter to Mrs. Stevens on the school bus, I hadn't heard this many words out of Ida Mae since the day she asked me if I wanted to be her friend. She looked at me hopefully. Mrs. Ruth looked at me hopefully, too.

"Okay," I finally said. "I'll see you around six."

"Great!" Ida Mae said.

"We'll see you then," her mother said.

They waved and turned to walk away when I suddenly realized I would need a present for Ida Mae. It was her birthday after all. I couldn't really afford anything, but my gut said I should. Just as I was starting to think about it, I noticed Mrs. Ruth speak to Ida Mae, then turn and walk rapidly toward me. "Beth," she said when she was near.

"Yes?"

"Don't bother with a present, dear. Ida Mae is our only child right now, so we have plenty of things for her birthday. The only thing we can't give her seems to be friends, so having you over will be the best present she could possibly have."

"Oh, okay . . ." I said, unsure what else I could say.

"See you this evening," Mrs. Ruth said, then hurried to catch up to Ida Mae.

Well, one problem down, I thought as I hurried from the mall.

On my way back toward the K.O.A. campground, I noticed a big sign: Thrift Shop. Perfect. An hour later, I emerged, my arms weighed down with plastic grocery sacks filled with two tops, three sweaters, a pair of jeans, and a skirt—I never knew when there might be a need for one. I was wearing a light jacket and had a heavier winter coat slung over my arm. The whole lot cost me less than fifteen dollars. It was enough to get me through, at least for awhile. I figured I could still use my other clothes. Throw a sweater over a top, and I was ready to go.

I hurried home. It was already going on five and I didn't want to be late for Ida Mae's party. She tried hard to be nice to me, and I'd been so withdrawn from her that I felt I owed it to her to come. I figured I'd have to take my chances with Mr. and Mrs. Ruth. Her mother seemed nice enough.

Surely one little party couldn't do too much harm. Besides, the promise of cake and ice cream sounded like a pretty good meal to me.

10

Ida Mae pulled the door open before the bell even had time to ring. "Come on in," she said as she swung the door wide. I stepped inside. The rich smell of chocolate cake in the oven filled the room, making my mouth water. I suddenly missed home and my mother.

"Thanks for coming," Ida Mae said. She didn't seem to notice that I wiped a tear from my face, or if she did, she was nice enough not to mention it. I remembered when I had seen her cry the day of Jill Kimball's birthday party. Ida Mae's party certainly didn't compare.

"Mother is icing the cake. Come on in and say hello." She urged me to follow her through the living room. The kitchen was warm from the oven. A table bearing four place settings sat in the center of the room, just a few steps from the countertop where Mrs. Ruth stood, adding the final touches of icing to Ida Mae's birthday cake.

"Glad you could come, Beth," Mrs. Ruth said. "I hope you like chocolate cake."

"It's my favorite."

"I forgot to mention we would have dinner first," she said. "I hope you're hungry."

"Yes, ma'am." I hadn't eaten anything since lunch, hoping the cake and ice cream would suffice for an evening meal. If it didn't, I had a couple of cans of vegetables at the shed for emergencies.

"Make yourself at home. Mr. Ruth will be here in just a few minutes and the party will begin," Mrs. Ruth said as she counted out thirteen candles to place on the cake. Twelve. My twelfth birthday had been just a few weeks before I left home for good. Mom forgot all about it, I guess, because she didn't even wish me *Happy Birthday*. I didn't expect Mark or Ryan to say anything, but I was disappointed Mom didn't.

I wonder if Mom even misses me, I thought. She might be happy I was able to get away. Maybe even envious. I wonder if she found Dad to tell him I'd gone? Probably not. She didn't have a clue where he was.

"Come down to the family room." Ida Mae interrupted my train of thought, saving me from the depression that was sure to come when I thought about Mom.

The first thing which struck me about Ida Mae's family room was the wall filled with pictures. You couldn't miss it. There must have been thirty eight-by-ten inch portraits hanging on the wall. I looked at them while Ida Mae fiddled near the stereo.

"Wanna listen to a CD?" she asked.

"Sure," I said.

The pictures were all of children—babies, toddlers, and kids a little older, more around our age. I searched for Ida Mae among them. I finally found her with the group who looked like they were in about fourth grade. Her face looked about the same as now, those freckles still popping out across her cheek bones. But her eyes seemed different. She looked scared in the photograph, sort of hollow, like my mom's eyes. Ida Mae didn't look a thing like any of the other kids whose photos were displayed.

"Hey, who are all these kids?" I asked, unable to keep my curiosity in check.

"My foster brothers and sisters, except some of them were here before I came, so I only know them by name."

"Foster? Why?" I had heard of the foster care system once at my old school when a new student moved into my class.

She closed the sliding door that carried the CD into the player. "They had to for different reasons. They came here to live with Mom and Dad until they could go back home or be adopted," she said.

"Adopted?" I was still confused.

"Yeah, adopted, just like me."

The music started to play automatically. "You're adopted?"

"Yep. And it's a good thing, too." Ida Mae's voice was matter-of-fact, like she had told this story before.

I sounded like an idiot, but I couldn't stop myself from asking, "Why would you say that?"

"Mom and Dad Ruth are great parents. I've been living with them now for three years. My birth parents weren't always so great," she said as she moved her head to the music. It was a group I recognized from before I left home,

52

but the song was new to me. "Birthday present," Ida Mae said as she nodded toward the CD player.

"I like it. What do you mean about your birth parents not being so great?" I asked, thinking of my own experiences, especially with Mark and Ryan.

"Aw, let's talk about it another day," Ida Mae said. "It's my birthday and I want it to be happy."

"Okay," I said. I really wanted to hear more about Ida Mae's family, and this foster thing, but I totally understood not wanting to talk about things. If I pried too hard, she might start asking me questions that I didn't want to answer either.

"Ida Mae," Mrs. Ruth said from the kitchen. "Your father is home."

"Come on. Let's go," Ida Mae said, as she stopped the CD and headed back toward the kitchen.

I followed. Mrs. Ruth was kissing a man, Ida Mae's father—adopted father, I corrected myself. Now I understood why Ida Mae didn't seem to look like either one of her parents. It had been a long time since I'd seen a couple look that happy.

"Dad, this is my friend Beth Burton." Ida Mae plopped onto a stool by the counter where the cake was sitting.

"Top of the evenin' to ya, Miss Burton," Ida Mae's father said. He stuck out his hand to give mine a firm shake.

"Nice to meet you, Mr. Ruth." He was nothing like

Mark, dressed like he'd just come from an office somewhere. I'd never seen Mark in a suit, or even wearing something that didn't look like he was enjoying yet another day off, sitting around drinking a beer. Mr. Ruth probably had never tasted a beer in his life.

"You girls go wash up now," Mrs. Ruth said. "Dinner is ready."

Ida Mae led the way to the bathroom at the top of the living room stairs. We scrubbed our hands, and I took an extra look in the mirror above the sink to check my face. I passed my own inspection and followed her down the stairs to the table.

"Ida Mae gets to sit at the head of the table tonight as the honored birthday girl," Mr. Ruth said. "Beth, how about you taking the chair to her right?"

"Sure," I said and slipped into the seat. Mr. Ruth helped his wife carry the food to the table. I hadn't seen so much warm food in one place in a long time—school lunches didn't count. Even when I was home with Mom there hadn't been anything much beyond fast food and sandwiches for several months.

"Don't be shy now," Mrs. Ruth said, encouraging me to fill my plate. "There is plenty for everyone. I'm used to cooking for a much bigger brood." I took a piece of meatloaf, two servings of mashed potatoes, which I covered in gravy, and a few green beans.

For the next few minutes, I mostly ate. I couldn't

believe how good the food tasted. All those months with only cafeteria food had made me forget how great a real, home cooked meal could be. Ida Mae and her parents talked about their day, while I continued to shovel food into my mouth.

When dinner was over, I helped carry the plates to the sink where Mrs. Ruth rinsed them off and Mr. Ruth loaded them into the dishwasher. Once the kitchen was put back in order, Mr. Ruth said, "It's present time."

The four of us trooped into the living room once again. Mrs. Ruth went directly to a closet where she retrieved the packages and carried them to the couch where Ida Mae and I sat. Ida Mae opened her packages and *oohed* and *ahhed* over everything. There were several pieces of new clothing, a diary, and another new CD for the player she had already shown me.

"Thanks, Mom and Dad," Ida Mae said as she jumped from her seat and ran to give them each a hug. I wished I could have a hug, too, and I had to fight tears back for the second time.

"Let's go listen to my new CDs," Ida Mae said.

"Okay," I said, as we excused ourselves.

"I'm glad Ida Mae has found a new friend," I heard her mother say just before I was out of range.

"Me, too," her father said.

***

Somehow Ida Mae and I lost track of the time, and the

next thing I knew, it was really dark outside. Mr. Ruth popped his head into the family room. "Ida Mae, it's getting close to bedtime."

"Oh," I said. "I didn't mean to stay so late."

"That's okay," Mr. Ruth said. "Did your mother expect you home tonight? You're welcome to spend the night, if you want." I noticed a look of concern flash across Ida Mae's face, just like I had earlier at the mall.

"Well, I . . ."

Mrs. Ruth joined us. "Why don't you give your mother a call and let her know you're just going to stay?"

I made a hasty decision. I wasn't sure why Ida Mae looked so concerned, but her parents sure didn't seem to mind. I was feeling welcomed in this home and the nights were getting colder in my shed. "She won't mind. I told her I might stay."

"Good!" Mrs. Ruth said.

"Well, goodnight, then," Mr. Ruth said as he left the room.

Even Ida Mae said, "I'm glad you can stay over, Beth," but she didn't much look like she meant it.

"Come on, girls," Mrs. Ruth said. "We'll get you settled in for the night." She led the way to Ida Mae's bedroom—I could tell it was hers from the books on her desk. A set of twin beds sat across from each other. "There are plenty of extra T-shirts to sleep in, Beth. Take your pick from the chest over there."

"Thanks," I said, as I heard Mrs. Ruth whisper to Ida Mae, "Don't worry. I'll be in to check on you." Then she spoke louder as she said, "Good-night, girls." She kissed Ida Mae on the cheek and patted the top of my head.

Soon we were each in our own bed. *Comfortable*, I thought. It had been a long emotional day for me, and I was tired. Ida Mae was too because she only said, "Thanks for coming to my party, Beth. Sleep tight."

"You, too, Ida Mae." I turned over on my side and soon fell fast asleep.

11

At some time during the night, I heard Mrs. Ruth come into the room and softly call Ida Mae's name. Ida Mae sat up in bed and mumbled a few groggy words. Her mother helped her from the room.

A few minutes later I heard the toilet flush, and Mrs. Ruth guided Ida Mae back into her bed before again leaving the room. In seconds, Ida Mae's breathing was back to a slow, steady rhythm.

The night sounds in the Ruth household were strange to me, yet somehow familiar. The clicking noise of a clock as the hands moved, the hum of a scented nightlight near the baseboard, the distant voices from a television off in another part of the house. Ida Mae's parents must have been watching one of the late night shows, Leno or Letterman I'd guess, unless it was already too late. I remembered my own mother stealing into my room in the middle of the night to check on me, rearrange my covers, or give me a kiss on the cheek when she thought I was sleeping. The thought struck me how lonely I had been, living alone in my shed.

I missed my mom. I wondered what she was doing. Did she miss me as much as I missed her? Mom had lost any fight since Dad left. Mark told her what to do, and, if she didn't respond quickly enough, he gave her a bruise to remind her. I doubted she had been able to get rid of him. It worried me to think I might someday see her name in the obituaries because he had killed her.

I watched the paper whenever I could, but it wasn't always easy. The school library only got the local newspaper. Sometimes it gave news from elsewhere in the county, but not always. The public library picked up several papers from the area, but I didn't get down there every day to read it, and they only kept the papers a day or two. I did read a note in the Police Beat that a twelve-year-old girl had been reported missing. I assumed it was me. The police were investigating, but no leads had come in. I doubted they would. I'd been careful not to let anyone know what I was planning. Mark was probably furious about the money I had stolen from him, but I didn't care. I wondered if the police would think to check the schools. Doubtful.

I had wanted to tell Mom my plans. I wanted to tell her everything, but I couldn't bring myself to tell her about Ryan. Her heart had been broken enough when Dad left. I couldn't let her know what a monster she invited to live with us. Mom wouldn't be the kind to go on TV and beg for me to return. I remembered several times when mothers were featured on the news and Mom said, "I bet they killed their own baby" and they had. She wouldn't want to bring that sort of suspicion and investigation into her own life, not after all she had been through. She would suffer silently that her daughter was a statistic, another child runaway.

I bet she thought I'd gone far, far away, like to Chicago or New York. That's the sort of garbage all the movies-of-the-week tried to make people believe. Gone off to find my way in the big city. Boy, would Mom be surprised to know I was in the county. There was no way I could let her know, not without the possibility of someone making me go back. I was sure they would never believe me if I told them about Ryan. Mark wouldn't believe me if I told him anything, because he was Ryan's father. Mom wouldn't believe he touched me because she would be afraid of losing Mark. Of course, she had already lost me, but I maybe I reminded her too much of Dad and she didn't mind.

Don't think about it, I tried to tell myself, hoping I would go back to sleep. My thoughts drifted to Ida Mae and her mother and all those photos hanging on the living room wall.

Ida Mae was adopted. Who would have guessed?

I knew Ida Mae could be annoying with all her chatter, but she really was a nice girl once you got to know her. I began to wonder why she didn't have any friends at school. No one ever talked with her. But now, there would be me. At least, Ida Mae would have me. And I would have her. Then, neither one of us would be quite so alone.

I drifted back to sleep, a smile on my face.

12

Monday I met Ida Mae at the bus stop.

"Hi," Ida Mae said as I neared where she stood.

I made sure the others saw we were standing together. "Good morning. Thanks again for having me over to spend the night Saturday. Your birthday cake was great." This brought a look of shock to the other faces, and the kids immediately began whispering and pointing their fingers at us. Ida Mae looked self-conscious. I shrugged it off.

I guess I was getting a little more secure. I'd been living in my shed for nearly three months and no one seemed to be the wiser. I thought I'd be able to make it through the winter now, too. I'd spent some money yesterday and bought a space heater for the shed. It was just the right size to keep my quarters warm and toasty. The shed was near enough to an electrical plug meant for campers to use, but I needed a weather-proof extension cord.

Ida Mae's mother had insisted I take home an afghan I admired after my stay. "You must," she said, "as a present from me."

I muttered my thanks, embarrassed that I needed just such a blanket so badly I couldn't refuse the generous offer. I could only hope she didn't figure out why.

After much shuffling, whispering, and pointing, Karly

Kincaide walked over to where Ida Mae and I were. Karly is in the same class we have with Jill Kimball, and they were best friends. Jill stood in the middle of the other students waiting for the bus to arrive.

"Go on," Jill said to Karly. "Ask her."

I gave Karly my best cold, hard stare. I knew whatever Jill had put her up to was probably no good, and I didn't really want to talk with any of them. Neither did Ida Mae. She sank down as far inside her coat as she could go without suffocating from the lack of air.

I decided to hit Karly head on. "Ask who what?"

Karly started to retreat, probably surprised I actually spoke to her.

"Go on, Karly," Jill said again.

I turned to her instead. "Why don't you just ask it yourself, Jill?" I said.

After a moment's hesitation, she stuck out her jaw in determination, "Okay, I will. I'm not afraid of either one of you." Her feet stayed planted where they were, but her body leaned toward me, as though she wanted to physically attack, but didn't have the guts.

"That's good to know," I said. "Since I'm not afraid of you either." This stopped Jill for a minute, pushing her back as though I'd hit her. Karly rejoined the crowd. Strength in numbers, I thought.

"You spent the night with Ida Mae?" Jill finally said.

I narrowed my eyes into slits, staring straight at Jill.

"Yeah. Something wrong with that?" I couldn't keep the defiance out of my voice.

"Did she pee her pants in the middle of the night?" Jill said.

"What?" I asked, trying not to laugh at her question. Then I remembered Mrs. Ruth coming into the bedroom, waking Ida Mae just enough to walk her to the bathroom. Ida Mae still wet her bed. I didn't see anything especially wrong with it. There were nights I'd been so sound asleep I barely woke in time to make it to the bathroom. So what? But I could see it bothered Ida Mae to have me find out.

"No, she didn't," I said.

"Well, I'm warning you. Don't sit on the same seat with her, and, if you insist on staying over at her house, don't sleep in the same bed, unless you want to get wet," Jill said.

I glanced toward Ida Mae then stepped closer. The bus was coming. Ida Mae was the only friend I had, and Jill deserved to know how it felt to be teased. Then I remembered the day of Ms. Meyers. Through my own haze of shock, I had seen Jill, sitting in her seat while all the others stood, trying to get one last look at Ms. Meyers. Jill's face was blank, her eyes glazed. I knew that look. I knew it, and still I was compelled as I asked, "And what sort of dirty little secrets are *you* keeping, Jill?" just as the bus rolled to a stop.

Jill stood with her mouth hanging open. I didn't know

what she was hiding, but she must have a good one. It was a mean thing to do, and, if someone asked me the same question, I would be standing with my mouth hanging open, too, not knowing what to say. I understood Jill Kimball much more than she wanted me to, but I had to protect Ida Mae.

The group stood stunned as Ida Mae and I climbed on the bus. Instead of taking my usual seat across the aisle, I slid in next to Ida Mae, who seemed grateful.

"Thanks," she said.

"No problem."

"Hey, you guys hurry up and get on the bus," Mrs. Stevens said.

Jill boarded the bus, along with Karly and the others. I stared at them all, daring them to say anything more to Ida Mae. Not one of them would even look at me.

This was the second time I'd come to someone's rescue since I had arrived. It felt sort of good. I knew Ida Mae had secrets. She still hadn't told me about her real parents and why she didn't live with them anymore. No one knew anything more about Ms. Meyers, but there had been a lot of speculation. I knew Jill Kimball had a story, and I had some clues as to what hers might be.

Now I knew why Ida Mae hesitated when her mother asked me to stay the night. It must have happened before, and Jill or some of her friends had been there. Heck, Ida Mae had lived with the Ruth family for three years. It could all be ancient history—although I doubted it, based on the way Ida Mae hid her face this morning. In any case, Little Miss Jill Kimball didn't need to be spreading the word to anyone new, ruining all chances Ida Mae had of making a friend. Ida Mae had a friend now. And it was me.

13

Jill Kimball might think herself the queen of all rumors, but somehow she let the best one of all slip past her this morning in her efforts to ruin a friendship for Ida Mae. By mid-morning, I heard Ms. Meyers was back at work. The event on the school bus was replayed in a hundred different ways by the time lunch period rolled around. Students who didn't ride that bus had their own versions to tell.

Rumors have a way of growing, which is really quite remarkable when you think about it. To hear kids talk, every one of them had seen Ms. Meyers with their own eyes and they had been the one to cover her up with the blanket. Well, it was fine by me. Let them think they were the ones to come to her aid, as long as they forgot it was me. Anonymity was still the key to my success.

The lunch lines were longer today than I had ever seen them. I guess everyone in the school wanted to get a first-hand look at Ms. Meyers, now that she'd returned. She was in the hot lunch line instead of her usual snack line. Students gave up their candy bar and soda for a hot lunch, despite the fact today's menu promised corn dogs, the worst of the worst kind of meal. The line moved slowly, giving each kid time to look Ms. Meyers over carefully. No one spoke to her, though. It was like they were afraid of what might come out of her mouth. Or maybe they were afraid she would strip down right there in front of them. Some might have hoped she would. What a story they would have to tell. I had heard of a teacher in Scandinavia who had come to class naked to teach her students that we are all equal.

But Ms. Meyers just kept dishing out pears, slapping a few carrots sticks into a compartment, and trying to keep the corn dogs from rolling off the tray before it passed over the service bar. She seemed to be her old self, smiling at each student as he or she passed by. She didn't speak, but she wasn't scary-looking or anything. The whole thing still made me wonder, but my own past kept me from asking questions, or wanting to pry. After a few minutes it was my turn to pick up a tray.

"Hello, Ms. Meyers." I kept my voice steady and just above a whisper. I didn't want to scare her off.

"Hello." She sounded like a regular, non-crazy person to me.

"Nice to see you again." I might as well keep talking while I waited for her to finish with my tray, I thought.

"It's nice to be seen." She lifted the tray and set it on top of the service bar.

"See you tomorrow," I said as I picked up my tray, ready to take to a seat.

"You bet," I heard her say as I walked away. Not much of a conversation. Not much more than I had at the bus stop with Ida Mae. I hoped it was enough to let Ms. Meyers know she had at least one friend. Someone she could count on to not ask anything. Someone who still knew how to be friendly. Someone who didn't care about her past. Someone who could understand.

It was hard to find an empty seat in the lunch room with all the extra people, so I stood for a few minutes waiting for a place to open. Ida Mae didn't seem to be around. I didn't blame her for wanting to hide. I imagined she was embarrassed by Jill's blurting the bedwetting problem in front of me. I noticed all the kids had their eyes trained in Ms. Meyers' direction and the noise level was more subdued than usual. I couldn't stand their rudeness, so I took my tray and went into the courtyard to eat. The courtyard was boxed in on all four sides by the building, making it almost warm enough to consider comfortable on this particular day. I noticed someone was sitting there already when I arrived. The person was bundled in a coat and eating from a lunch tray. I recognized the coat. It was Ida Mae. I went over to join her. Figuring she had chosen the courtyard on purpose, I didn't say anything about her sitting out here alone. We ate quickly and returned our trays to the lunch line before she spoke.

"I need to spend the rest of lunch period in the library. Want to come with me?" She ducked her head, as though she were embarrassed that she even asked me.

"Sure," I said. The library was one of my favorite

places to hide, too, so I was right at home being there with Ida Mae. Usually I headed for the fiction shelves. I spent a lot of my alone time reading about people whose lives were better than mine. Of course, some stories didn't work out so well, but most of them did and it made me happy to know somehow things could be fine. But today—although I still didn't understand what possessed me—I moved toward the newspaper racks. I picked up the local paper and started flipping through the pages. A small headline caught my eye.

"Man Booked for Domestic Violence." I don't know how, but even before I read the police blotter entry, I knew it was Mark. I read through the piece once, then again, more slowly the second time. He had beaten his live-in girlfriend—my mother—enough to send her to the hospital with three broken ribs, a broken arm, and severe bruises on her cheek and nose. His sixteen-year-old son had been placed under protective custody—whatever that meant—and Mark would go to trial on abuse charges.

I dropped into my seat. The thoughts whirled around and around in my head so quickly I could hardly sort through them. Mom was in the hospital. She had three broken ribs, a broken arm, and bruises. I had to go to her. But what if Mark was set free before the trial? Mom had no gumption anymore. She couldn't make him stay away.

And what about *him*? What did *protective custody* mean?

I couldn't take the chance, even if Mom did need me. There was no mention of me or my disappearance. The reported missing twelve-year-old I had seen listed earlier hadn't been me, or they would have said something about it in the article. Maybe Mom had told people I was with my dad. That made sense. Otherwise the school truancy officials would have been looking for me.

Lunch period was almost over when I dug in my pocket and produced a coin. I took the newspaper over to the copy machine, dropped in my money, and waited for the hot sheet to come out of the feeder. I folded it into a neat square and slid it into my back pocket. I wanted solid proof Mom was going to be okay. I replaced the newspaper into the rack and went over to Ida Mae.

"Hey, are you okay?" she asked.

"Yeah. Why?" Guilt washed through me, but I tried not to let it show.

"You're pale."

"Just a little cold, that's all," I said, keeping my voice steady, normal. "The bell's ready to ring." I started out of the library, and she followed me.

With Mom in the hospital, and Mark in jail, I couldn't concentrate on school work the rest of the day.

14

"Mom's taking a new placement today," Ida Mae said when I arrived at the bus stop the next morning.

"What's that mean?" I asked, interested, but a little preoccupied. I still hadn't decided how to let Mom know I was okay without giving myself away.

"A new foster placement. There's a teenage boy coming to stay at our house for awhile."

"That's nice," I said, my mind still not on what she was saying. It didn't matter to Ida Mae that I wasn't especially talkative this morning. Since I had spent the night at her house and became her regular bus riding companion, we slipped into an easy sort of friendship where Ida Mae did a lot of talking and I did a lot of listening. I didn't have to answer many questions, and I'd sort of learned to enjoy listening to her constant steady stream, even when I didn't understand some of the words she used about the foster-family thing.

"I'm not sure how I feel about having an older boy around the house," Ida Mae said. "We've never had a boy older than ten before. Mom said it would probably be just for a few weeks, but that's what she thought when I came, too, and look at me—they adopted me."

Adopted. That reminded me I wanted to find out more about Ida Mae's adoption. She had mentioned her birth parents weren't very good. I needed to take my mind off my own troubles for a little while anyway, if I wanted to get through the rest of the day without spilling my own secrets and heading back to my hometown to see my mom.

"Hey, Ida Mae," I said. I didn't want to sound too pushy, but I was interested, and she had said she'd tell me her story another time. This time was a good as any, I supposed.

"Yes?" Her voice sounded almost surprised I had something to say. I guess I really didn't talk with her as much as I should.

"You told me you were adopted. Were you once a placement with the Ruths?"

Ida Mae looked around at the others standing at the bus stop with us. Most of the kids were ignoring us like usual, but Karly and Jill were close enough they had probably heard Ida Mae say "teenage boy." They hung on to our every word.

"I'll tell you about it when we get on the bus," Ida Mae said. I nodded my understanding. Mrs. Stevens brought the bus to a squealing halt just a few minutes later.

"They really ought to do something about the noise those brakes make," I said to Mrs. Stevens when I climbed into my usual seat next to Ida Mae.

"What noise?" Mrs. Stevens asked, as she pulled the bus door closed with a clang, and we were on our way. She had the CB radio delivering static loud enough to almost drown out the country music from the regular radio, although I couldn't figure out the song over the deafening roar.

Jill and Karly left us for their usual seats near the back. Two boys had the seat behind us. They were elementary age and too wrapped up in their card collections to care what we were talking about.

"I've been Ida Mae Ruth now for only a year, but I've lived with Mother and Dad Ruth for nearly three," Ida Mae said without further prompting. "I was a mess when I first came. A broken arm, two broken ribs, and lots of bruises."

Just like my mom, I thought. Ida Mae kept talking, unaware I suddenly had someone else on my mind.

"I was real skinny from not getting much food. My dad liked to beat up on both me and my mom whenever he could, but this was the first time either one of us had ever ended up in the hospital."

I had a vision of my own mother, lying at this very minute in a bed following a beating from Mark. I understood how Ida Mae's dad had been. I knew how her mother must have kept those beatings a secret and made Ida Mae, too. Mom and I had done the same thing ourselves. Three years since Mark and Ryan came. Three years since Ida Mae came to live with the Ruth family. I felt closer to Ida Mae than ever before. We had something in common. Something not nice. Something not pretty. Something most people did not, could not, would not understand.

Ida Mae went on with her story. "My mom called 9-1-1 and the ambulance came. They brought the police. I didn't remember much after that for a day or two. Mom and Dad Ruth have filled in some details for me." She looked up to see if I was still interested in her story. It was hard for me to hide the truth showing in my eyes. "The police hauled my dad into jail and Family Services decided I'd be better off in a foster home. I came to stay with the Ruths. My mother refused to leave him." Ida Mae lowered her face. "He didn't have to track her down. Just as soon as they let him out of jail, he went back to our trailer and killed her. Pulled out his shotgun and killed her."

I didn't know what to say.

"He was sentenced to life. He might be out already for all I know. The courts decided he could never have me back, though, and the Ruths asked to adopt me. It took awhile for everything to go through, but I never have to see him again."

"Oh, Ida Mae," I said. "I'm so sorry." And I meant it. Her story had been like mine to a point, but my mom was at least still alive. Poor Ida Mae had lost everything.

"Don't be," she said. "The Ruths are wonderful, and I love them. I miss my mom, but I know she wouldn't have been able to really take care of me. She was too afraid of him. He beat us a lot, and she never did a thing. Sometimes I'd be sound asleep, and he'd come in drunk and rip me from my bed to start beating me. I had bad dreams and was

74

always afraid." Ida Mae's voice dropped so low I could barely make out the next few words. "That's why I sometimes wet the bed."

I thought I understood it all now. I looked toward the back of the bus. Jill Kimball was chatting away about something from her own insignificant world. I continued to stare. After a few minutes, I caught Jill's eye. She snapped her mouth closed, then slid farther into her seat. Her friends were oblivious. I watched her all the way to school. When the bus ground to a halt, I let Ida Mae slip past me.

"See you inside," I said and she nodded. I stood, waiting. Jill Kimball refused to look my way as she passed, but I know she heard me. "You've been hurt yourself. How can you be so mean?" Jill hurried into the school. I followed a short distance behind.

15

Although it really wasn't spring, the weather didn't seem to realize it this morning. The temperatures were higher than they had been in weeks and the morning sun burned off the last clumps of snow from two weeks ago. The winter months had passed quickly, and I had made it fairly well in my campground shed, thanks to a mild season. Only a few more weeks of winter. I knew I could make it until the end of school. After that, I wasn't sure what I would do. Campers would start showing up once Memorial Day arrived. I needed to keep my home a secret in case I had to use it again next fall.

As if housing wasn't enough for me to worry about, I still didn't know what to do about Mom. I wanted to let her know I was all right, as much as I wanted to find out if she was doing okay. Few details had been in the newspapers, which I now read regularly at school. I knew Mark was out of jail with a trial date set. Ryan was still in protective custody, something I needed to find out more about. Mom, I just didn't know. Her injuries had been bad, but not serious enough to warrant keeping her in the hospital more than overnight. Had she kicked Mark out of the apartment and moved back in herself? Or was he still living there with her, despite the pending court date?

Poor Mom. I guess I was feeling a little more lonely

than usual. I hadn't been to Ida Mae's house since the birthday party. I didn't want to invite myself. We had talked about it, but the Ruths were adjusting to the boy who had moved in with them from foster placement. I knew Ida Mae would ask me again once everything settled.

Ida Mae didn't have much to say about the new boy. He was four years older than her, so he probably made other friends. She called him Ryan, and the name alone gave me the creeps, so I didn't encourage her to talk about him. All I could think of was the other Ryan. I didn't want to be reminded.

Despite my mood, the bright sunshine lured me to walk downtown, basking in the spring-like warmth. I visited my favorite hangout, the library. I chose two books fresh from the publisher, and two non-fiction books to get me through the weekend. Other than missing Mom, the weekends and school vacations spent alone were the worst thing about my self-exile. Books provided comfort. I read everything, but my favorites were the classics. I'd already devoured most of Dickens and Robert Louis Stevenson, plus a few Shakespearian plays since I left home. Today, I picked up something modern, a Carol Lynch Williams and one by Cynthia Voigt, plus the non-fiction.

After the library, I wandered toward the market. I needed a pint of milk, a box of cereal, and some fruit for tomorrow morning. I didn't dare buy more than a pint of milk now that the sun was shining. I'd learned the hard way last fall when the half gallon I bought turned sour while I was at school. The shed smelled bad for days. I was afraid the odor would get into my clothes, and people would think it was me that smelled rotten.

I was glad to put my knapsack into the shopping cart for a few minutes as I wheeled it through the store. I wasn't looking forward to the long walk home, carrying my books and the added groceries, but I didn't have much choice. The city bus didn't run on Saturday. I stood poking at the plums, trying to decide if they were ripe enough to eat, when I heard a familiar voice.

"Hello." I looked up to see Ms. Meyers standing next to me. She had on a pale blue T-shirt and jeans. Her hair was combed down and her face wore no make-up. She smiled at me and I smiled back.

"Hello," I said.

"It's Beth, isn't it?"

"Yes. That's what I go by." I'd actually gotten so used to being Beth Burton now my real name seemed far, far away. Liz, Lizbeth, Beth—all short for Elizabeth, the name my mother gave me.

"Is it short for Elizabeth?" Ms. Meyers asked.

It was like she'd been reading my mind. "Yes," I said. "But I prefer Beth."

"Beth it is, then," Ms. Meyers said. I noticed a faint blush come to her cheeks.

"Yes," I said. No one had found out the real reasons

why she ran that day that I knew of. Other than a few "Hellos" in the lunch line, it was the only contact I ever had with Ms. Meyers. Until now.

"Beth," she began again. "I've never really thanked you for . . . what you . . . did."

"You don't need to . . ." I wanted to let her off the hook.

"I do. I need to thank you for trying to protect me, to protect my dignity, although I didn't have much left." She smiled at me. "I'd gotten myself into a real mess then, but life is going much better now."

"I'm glad," I said. So was mine.

"Me, too," she said, relief obvious in her voice. Then, almost to herself, she said, "It's funny how we can get ourselves into tight places and not know how to get out. Sometimes we need to be rescued."

I knew how she felt, but I was surprised to hear it come from an adult. Didn't only kids needed to be rescued? Then it struck me. Mom needed rescuing. She hadn't been able to get out and Mark had sent her to the hospital. She hadn't escaped like I had. There were times I wanted to tell the truth so bad I thought I would pop. I'd written papers for school I had to tear up, said things to Ida Mae that I thought she'd figure out my secret for sure. I'd felt like pouring my soul out to Mrs. Ruth the night I stayed over. Now, talking with Ms. Meyers, the same urge to tell all came bubbling to the surface. Somehow, I thought she might be the perfect one to understand.

"So," she said. I could tell she was ready to change the subject. "If you have your shopping done, would you like a ride home? I don't know where you live, but it must be somewhere near me since that's the bus you ride." The blush returned to her cheek.

I always seemed to surprise myself, and today was no exception. "Sure," I said, then wondered how I was going to avoid her finding out my *home* was a shed at the K.O.A. We both went through the check-out, and I picked up the shoulder-bag holding my library books before I followed Ms. Meyers out to her car. We loaded up and were on our way.

The conversation was light and easy, and I soon felt comfortable with Ms. Meyers. She asked me about the school year, and I felt safe in answering the questions. She acted really interested in what I had to say. I liked Ms. Meyers. I thought she liked me. And, I was glad I helped her when she most needed it. Somehow I knew she would be there if I ever needed her help in return.

I soon realized we were almost at her house. "You can let me out at your house, and I'll walk the rest of the way home," I said.

"No, that's okay."

"Really. It's only a couple more blocks, and it's been such a nice day, I'd like to walk." I couldn't let her get any closer to my camp. No houses surrounded the parking area, and if I told her I lived in one of the houses close to her place, she'd know I wasn't telling the truth. Walking from here was safer.

She pulled into her driveway. "Well, if you insist." She chuckled.

"I do." I popped out of the car, but leaned back in before Ms. Meyers could unhook her seat belt. "Thanks for the ride. I'll see you at school on Monday."

"See you then, Beth," she said.

I slipped around the nearby corner so she wouldn't see which way I had gone. I headed toward my shed, content I had made a friend, but thinking about what Ms. Meyers said. *Sometimes we need to be rescued.* I remembered something Mom once told me—another one of her Elizabeth-quotes: "Elizabeth Taylor said that Vivian Leigh was her heroine, innocence on the verge of decadence, always there to be saved."

Was that it? Was mom an innocent, always needing to be saved? Where did that leave me? Was I just like her, or would I be the one who had to do the rescuing?

16

As usual, the following Saturday morning found me walking toward town, bag of library books in tow and a shopping list mentally prepared. The spring days were getting warmer, and the walk was invigorating. It felt good to be alive, a much different feeling from that I had a year ago.

After my stop at the library, I headed to the market where I picked up the few items I knew I would need. On my way to the checkout, I came to an abrupt halt. A new display stood in the middle of the aisle. Postcards! Postcards advertising sights from all over the state and beyond. The idea flashed through my mind with lightening speed. I could send my mom a postcard from somewhere else. She'd know I was all right, but the card face would lead her to a location far, far away. The idea was perfect. I selected a card from out-of-state. Might as well make it really far away, and paid for it with my groceries.

"Got any stamps around here?" I asked the cashier.

"Over by the door." She pointed then turned to wait on the next person in line behind me.

I dug some lose change from my jeans pocket and walked to the automatic stamp machine at the front of the store. I'd never noticed it before, or I might have had this plan a long time ago. I dropped in the correct amount, and a

Lu Ann Brobst Staheli

clear plastic sleeve popped out, a first-class stamp enclosed. I peeled the stamp from the holder and stuck it right onto the little square on the postcard, afraid I'd lose it on my way to a mailbox if it wasn't already attached.

"Shoot!" I said aloud to myself when I realized I didn't have a pen or pencil on me. I'd have to walk all the way back into town again this morning if I wanted to mail the card today. Or I'd have to wait until Monday. No use sending the card on Sunday since the mail wouldn't be picked up anyway. I started to walk toward the campground, resigning myself to the second trip.

"Beth! Beth!" I heard Ida Mae call my name from nearly a block away. She was standing in her front yard, waving her hand in the air as she called to me.

"Hi, Ida Mae," I said as I returned her wave. I continued walking toward her, aware of how heavy my book bag and grocery sack were getting to be.

"What'cha got in there?" Ida Mae asked, pointing at my grocery bag.

"Just a few things from the store."

"Couldn't your mom give you a ride?" Ida Mae asked.

Mom had been on my mind this morning, as she had been all week that I almost blew my cover, but stopped myself in time. "No. She had to run out of town for the day and asked me if I'd mind."

"My mother's gone today, too," said Ida Mae. "She had to take Ryan to Family Services for a meeting with his dad. Want to come in for awhile? We could grab a bite to eat."

Lunch sounded good to me. My apple from breakfast had long since worn thin under the exertion of walking to and from town, especially loaded down. "I'd love it," I said, smiling at Ida Mae with a full-faced grin.

"Come on," she said as we headed into the house. "Anything in the sack that's going to melt?" Ida Mae asked when we made our way into the kitchen.

"No, but I do have some milk." I remembered Mom telling me when I was a little kid that the calcium was good for me. Now that I had been on my own, I worked hard to get all the vitamins I might need. I had to stay healthy.

"How does a cheese sandwich sound?" Ida Mae said, her head poking into the opened fridge.

"Great," I said. I took my milk carton from the paper bag and set it on the shelf in front of her, hoping Ida Mae didn't ask why it was so tiny.

Ida Mae assembled the cheese sandwich and set one on each of the two plates she took from the cupboard shelf. She found a half-eaten bag of potato chips. "They might be stale," she said as she put some on the plates, then handed one to me.

"Once a potato chip, always a potato chip," I said, and she laughed.

"Soda?"

"If it's okay with your mom," I said, not wanting to

84

make Mrs. Ruth upset with an unexpected guest drinking the last one.

"She won't care. She always keeps extra on hand. You never know when we might get another permanent house guest around this place."

Once we finished our meal, I helped Ida Mae wipe down the dishes we used and put them away. I glanced at the clock and realized I wouldn't have time to go all the way to my shed, write the note to my mom, and make it back to the post office box. I might make today's mail though, if I borrowed a pen from Ida Mae and left my bags here until I could run downtown, then back.

"Ida Mae, do you think I could borrow a pen? I need to write a quick message on a postcard and get it on its way."

"No problem," she said as she started to rummage through a desk drawer, then scribbled several pens against a pad of paper until she found one that worked. "Who are you sending it to?"

"Thanks," I said, trying to hold back my tongue from spilling the truth as I carefully began to write my mom's address—my former address—on the card.

"One of your old friends?"

"Yes," I said, hoping she wouldn't pry any further. She didn't.

Dear Mom, I wrote. *I'm okay. Love, Liz.* I wanted to tell her I'd read about her in the paper, but didn't know how far away they would cover Mark's being hauled in. I couldn't take the chance, so this short message would have to do.

"Want to run down to the post office with me?" I asked Ida Mae.

"Sure. Let me just go make sure the cat's been let out."

"I want to make today's mail, so try to hurry, okay?"

"Be right back," Ida Mae said as she ran out of the room.

I wandered into the living room to give those photos on the wall another glance. I quickly located Ida Mae and scanned the other nearby photos. Some of them were old, others looked fairly new. The girl in the picture hanging next to the one of Ida Mae looked familiar. It was taken so long ago, I couldn't be sure.

Was it really Jill Kimball? Surely Ida Mae would have said something to me. I vowed to ask her about the photo once we were on our way.

"Ready?" Ida Mae said from the doorway.

"You bet," I said as I started toward her. I glanced at the last of the photographs. It was brand new. This boy, too, looked familiar. It couldn't be! I stopped and went back to give the photograph a closer look. Hanging right here on the wall at Ida Mae's, a picture of my own abuser? Mark's wicked son? Was Ida Mae's foster brother Ryan the same Ryan I had run from?

"Are you okay?" Ida Mae said as she touched her hand against my arm. I jumped and started to back away until I realized it was her. "You turned white as a sheet," she said, but my ears were burning, and the ringing was so loud I could hardly hear her.

"We have to get away," I whispered. I pulled loose from her touch and started to run.

I wasn't sure where at first, but I knew I had to get away. Away from the photo. Away from Ida Mae's house. Away from Ryan. What if he came home? What if he saw me? What if he touched me?

I could hear Ida Mae's footsteps following close behind, but I didn't slow down.

I ran the way Ms. Meyers had run, not seeing where I was going, not caring who was behind me, just knowing I had to escape. But who would be there to save me?

Somehow I made it to the mail drop box. I almost crashed into it before I could come to a stop. Without thinking, I slammed my postcard down the slot then let the door clang shut. There, I'd done it. At least Mom would know I'd been safe. But Ryan was at Ida Mae's house. I was no longer safe. And neither was Ida Mae.

I had to save her, and the only way I knew how was to stop trying to save myself.

17

I stood leaning against the mailbox, panting for breath when Ida Mae caught up to me.

"Hey, what's wrong with you?" she asked.

"It's *him*," I said, but Ida Mae immediately interrupted.

"There's my mom and Ryan coming up the road. Let's flag her down and catch a ride." Ida Mae started waving like crazy.

"No!" I said. I didn't take the time to look Mrs. Ruth's way. I had to escape before he could see me.

"Beth!" Ida Mae yelled as I darted away.

I could only hope she would be okay with her mother there with her. Please don't let her be alone in the house with him, I prayed as I headed toward the K.O.A. Once I was in my bed and calmed down, I gradually realized the mistakes I had just made.

First off, I was hungry, and all my weekend supplies were at Ida Mae's house where I had left them. Second, I hadn't gotten through to her that Ryan—the same Ryan staying at her house—was the reason I had to run away, a thing she didn't even know about, except for when I ran today. Third, running away from home and covering the truth with lies might have seemed like the answer, but now I could see it wasn't.

Home! My mother. Oh, no! I thought. The postmark! I

never even thought until this very moment the postmark would be a dead giveaway. I had to get the card back, and then I had to tell Ida Mae the truth about my running away—all of my reasons for running away.

My growling stomach wouldn't let me move until I put something in it, so I opened a can of pork and beans. I huddled close to my space heater, hoping to make the chills I felt clear to my bones fade away. The temperatures had been so much warmer recently that I hadn't used the heater for several days. The heating element gave off a whiff of stale odor; something like a toaster with the bread stuck in too long, but the warmth renewed my spirit. I would be okay. I'd go to the post office and ask for my postcard back then I'd try to find a way to tell Ida Mae about Ryan and why I had run.

I looked at my watch and knew the post office was closed, but I struck out anyway, hoping someone would still be there, sorting the mail that had come in during the day. Since the town was not that big, I knew all the drop boxes must lead to one place, the city post office in the center of town. I hopped onto my bike this time, hurrying just in case someone there could help. I made sure to keep my eyes open and avoided Ida Mae's house on the way. No one was stirring when I rode past Ms. Meyers' house, and I couldn't decide if that was a good thing or not. I still had a sneaking suspicion she would understand what I was feeling. Ms. Meyers might even know some way to help me. But, I couldn't afford the time right now to stop and talk it over with her. Maybe later, I told myself.

I arrived at the post office and, as I figured, the door to the customer service window was locked. I listened for a few minutes in the lobby, just in case I could hear someone stuffing mail into the customer's private boxes. Nothing. I left the building and rounded the corner toward the loading dock. The lot was empty except for a dumpster filled with trash. I rang the service bell, but got no response. I pounded on the dock doors and tried to jump up high enough so I could see in the discolored windows at the top of each door. My mind told me there was no way I could jump that high, but my sudden overwhelming desperation made me give it a try. I had just been struck with how important getting the postcard back might be to both my own and my mother's safety. Ryan was here and the danger was much more real again to me.

No luck at seeing in the windows. No response to my knocking. Nothing. I sat down on the step for a few minutes, long enough for the events of the day to soak in and my worry to develop into feelings of hopelessness. I began to cry.

I lost track of how long I sat there. I was only mildly aware of the traffic going by on the street. I was startled when I heard my name.

"Beth?" It didn't sound like Ida Mae. "Beth Burton?" It definitely wasn't Mom. "Are you okay?" It wasn't Ms. Meyers' voice, either.

Lu Ann Brobst Staheli

I looked up through reddened eyes to see Jill Kimball standing directly in front of me, not five feet away. Of the people I knew from school, I certainly wouldn't have guessed Jill.

"Better," I said, fully expecting her to walk away. Of course, I also expected to hear a great tale at school about how I was bawling and wouldn't take any help when Jill offered it to me. Jill needed a new story since I'd embarrassed her at trying to tell long-ago tales about Ida Mae. Instead, she came and sat on the step next to me. She dug into her pocket and came out with a tissue. It appeared to be clean, even if it was wrinkled.

"Here," she said, offering it to me.

I took it and tried to wipe the last tears from my eyes, hoping I wasn't smearing any dirt across my face in the process. "Thanks." We both sat there silently for several minutes. I wasn't sure what to say. Here was the girl who so mercilessly picked on Ida Mae, sitting next to me, while I was filled with agony about how I to get out of this mess and protect myself, while also trying to protect Ida Mae.

"It's okay if you don't want to talk about it," Jill said. "I'll just sit here with you until you feel better."

I needed some sort of excuse, but I didn't want to tell her anything she could use against me. "I mailed a card today to my . . . my friend, and I forgot I had something more I wanted to say. I'm just frustrated I couldn't add a note to my message."

91

It was a good cover because Jill nodded her head, but I wasn't happy about what she had to say. "Mail's already gone for the day. It goes to the main post office in the state capitol, gets divvied up then it's on its way. Guess you'll have to send a new note on Monday."

I wasn't convinced she believed me. "Yeah. I guess so," I said. Then a hopeful thought struck. "If it goes to the state capitol first, does it get postmarked from there?" I asked.

"No, that's the last thing they do from here. Didn't your school take you on a trip to the post office last year to teach you all these things?"

"I guess I was absent that day," I said. I was absent a lot the final year at my old school because of the bruises. I didn't want anyone to see me and get suspicious. Who knew what Ryan might do to me, or what Mark might do to Mom if the secrets got out? I hadn't taken any chances, although now I wondered if maybe I should have done that, rather than run away. No, I thought. It's better this way. Mom got out with a few broken bones. With any luck, the judge will put Mark in prison.

But there's still Ryan. The thought raced through my mind. I had to concentrate on what Jill was saying and tried to ignore my own worries.

"You really didn't miss much of anything," she said as she rose from the step. "If there's ever anything I can do to help . . ."

I could hardly believe the offer. "Okay," I said, about to let her leave. Then a photograph popped into my mind. An image, of a younger girl, a photograph I had seen today on the living room wall at Ida Mae's. I had to ask. "Jill?"

"Yes?" she said, looking down at me from her standing place.

I almost abandoned my question but decided to press on. "Did you ever live with Ida Mae?" Jill's knees suddenly went weak. She slumped back onto the step beside me. "I've seen the photo. It hangs on the Ruths' family room wall. It's you, isn't it?"

Jill nodded her head. "Yes, it's me."

"You were a foster child, just like Ida Mae? You lived with the Ruth family?"

"Just until my mom stopped drinking and my step-dad moved away," she said.

I couldn't stop myself from asking. "Were you . . ." A look of panic swept across her face. "It's okay," I said. "I already know. I guess you're with your mother now?" Again she nodded. "I guess nobody knows."

"Nobody but Ida Mae and her family," Jill said. "I went back home shortly after I was taken away. Everyone thought it would be best to keep it quiet since my mother still wanted to live here with me. They didn't want people to gossip."

Here was the biggest gossip I knew telling me Ida Mae covered for her when she didn't have the same courtesy toward Ida Mae.

"I'm sorry I tried to hurt Ida Mae," Jill said.

"You shouldn't apologize to me," I said. "You should apologize to her."

"I'm not sure she would want to listen to me."

"You should at least give it a try." Jill nodded and gave a big sigh. "Thanks for sitting here with me," I said.

I had trouble hearing what she had to say in response. The entire city fire truck fleet immediately flipped on their sirens in the fire station next door, and trucks and cars began to roll. We stood for a moment and watched them tear down the street.

"Wonder where they're headed," Jill said.

"I don't know," I said, but a heavy feeling dropped into the pit of my stomach. They were headed away from downtown, toward the K.O.A. My shed! I suddenly remembered I had left on the space heater. The space heater that was giving off a funny smell earlier today. Please let my shed be okay, I chanted silently as I jumped up, grabbed my bike, and pedaled toward home. I heard Jill's footsteps halt not far into my escape. Then everything became a blur as I rode and rode and rode.

I could see the flames from two blocks away. Dropping my bike to the ground, and squeezing through bystanders who watched the fire, I moved as close as I could to see the last ashes of my shed fall away.

"Space heater and an old mattress," I heard the fire chief say. "And this doll."

Elizabeth Taylor had been burned to a crisp.

18

I had to leave, or my cover would be completely ruined. I ran blindly from the campgrounds. How could I be so stupid! I could not believe the disaster of this day.

Finally, exhausted from all my running from crisis to crisis, I collapsed on a grass parkway. I lost track of where I was, or near whose house I might be, until I heard my name. Then I knew. It was Mrs. Ruths' gentle voice calling out, "Beth." And suddenly I didn't want to run away any more. I wanted to tell her everything. I needed to tell her everything. I climbed into her open arms and began to sob for the second time today.

"Shhhh, shhhh," Mrs. Ruth said. "Everything will be fine." When my racking sobs turned to hiccups, Mrs. Ruth said, "Would you like to tell me about it now?"

I decided I couldn't go on this way. I couldn't let Ida Mae be in danger to protect me. I couldn't let my mom continue to worry. I couldn't continue to take care of me, especially since all my worldly possessions had just gone up in flames. I nodded *yes*.

"Then let's go into the house." She started to say more but I interrupted her.

"No!"

Mrs. Ruth was startled, but assured me again that everything was okay. I could tell she had lots of experience with kids my age, kids who had trauma in their lives, even trauma like mine. We continued to sit on the cool parkway, oblivious to the people who were returning to their homes after watching the fire.

"Wouldn't you like to come into the yard, Beth?" Mrs. Ruth said. "We don't have to go into the house if you don't want to, but I think the plastic chairs in the back yard might be more comfortable."

"Is Ryan still here?" I could hear the panic in my voice.

"Yes," she said, confusion evident on her face.

"Is Ida Mae in there alone with him?" I'd gone all high and squeaky as I fought the fears that were rushing around inside me.

A look of true concern crossed her eyes, but she said, "No."

"Good," I said, getting up from the lawn and leading the way to the backyard chairs.

Once I started to talk, I couldn't stop. The entire horrid story came pouring out, the way Ryan had abused me, the way his father treated my mother, the steps I took to run away, and the new life I had created living at the K.O.A. I told it all, every sordid detail, but not once did Mrs. Ruth interrupt me or look away. I knew she believed me, and somehow I knew she had heard it all before. When I was finished, she took my hand in hers.

"Everything will work out, Beth," she said then added, "Is Beth even your real name?"

"Elizabeth. Liz," I told her, glad to once again say my own real name.

"You wait here, Liz," Mrs. Ruth said. "Ryan is in the house, so I need to make a phone call before you come in. We'll get everything set right today."

"Okay," I said, concerned that he was so near, yet confident everything would be fine. Mrs. Ruth had promised, and I believed her.

Mrs. Ruth went to the back door, opened it, and called both her husband and Ida Mae to the door. I knew she was explaining a bit of what happened to me, but I couldn't hear her words. Almost immediately, Ida Mae rushed to my side and threw her arms around me.

"Mom will take care of everything," she said. Mr. Ruth stayed near the opened doorway, and Mrs. Ruth went inside.

A few minutes later I heard Mrs. Ruth call Ryan into the kitchen. Mr. Ruth stepped back inside. Ida Mae continued to sit beside me, just as Jill Kimball had done earlier, silently giving me support. We heard the garage door open and two car doors close before Mrs. Ruth came back outside.

"Ryan is going to the shelter to spend a few nights," she said. Ida Mae nodded. I didn't understand. Mrs. Ruth continued, "On Monday, we will meet with his foster worker after one meets with Beth, or Liz I should say."

"A foster worker is going to meet with me?" I asked. I

fought another moment of panic.

"Don't worry, Beth. They are A-okay," Ida Mae said.

"You'll stay here with us, at least until everything gets sorted out," Mrs. Ruth said. "Was the fire today the shed where you've been living?"

"Yes," I said. "I don't have much money left. Will I need to pay for the damage?"

"We'll work it out on Monday," Mrs. Ruth said. "Now, what about your mother? Should we go inside and give her a call and let her know you're safe?"

"Oh, yes," I said, knowing Mrs. Ruth and the foster worker would help Mom. I didn't need to worry about Mark or Ryan anymore.

I dialed the number, and Ida Mae and her mother slipped into the other room. But the telephone never rang. An electronic operator broke onto the line to inform me the number had been changed, and no further information was available. I struggled hard to hold back more tears. Mom was lost, and I was the one who had run away.

I rejoined Ida Mae and her mother in the kitchen. "Line isn't working," I said to their hopeful looks. "We'll track it down on Monday." I would be fine until then, and I needed some time to think.

They nodded and Ida Mae handed me a stack of plates. "Everyone pitches in around here," Ida Mae said.

"And it's my day to set the table, I see," I said, pleased to be a part of the Ruth family. Even if were only to be for a short while.

19

The second chest of drawers in Ida Mae's room had been empty when I first came upstairs, but now my arms were chock full of clothes pretty close to the right sizes for me.

Ida Mae had taken me to the *foster* room, she called it, where tubs filled with clothes of all sizes and seasons were stored for both boys and girls.

"Most kids come to stay with nothing, so Mom and Dad keep these on hand for whoever needs them," she said. "Here." Ida Mae shoved a plastic freezer bag at me, which I noticed was filled with a toothbrush, toothpaste, deodorant, soap, and other things a kid might need.

"Thanks," I said.

"No problem. Let me know if there's anything else you want," she said, as we trooped back into the bedroom to store my belongings.

"I left my bike over on the parkway, by the shed," I said, suddenly remembering the only possession I had left in the world.

"I'll take care of it," Ida Mae said. She must have known I needed some time to myself to think, because she slipped away while I was putting the clothing into a drawer she had indicated for my things.

She was a great friend. Just the thought Ryan had been

sleeping in a room near her gave me the chills. I knew what could have happened to her if she was ever alone in this house with him, and I felt guilty that I hadn't really done anything about him before. All I had done was protect myself by running away. I hurt my mom, I was sure. And by leaving her there, Mark hurt her, too, physically.

Ryan—I had to practice calling him that now. If I had called him by his name all along if I had told Ida Mae the truth like she told me—then this might not be happening now. He would have never been here in the house with her. Of course, I might not be either, and something deep inside told me I would be less of who I had become without this experience.

Once I was through putting away the stuff collected from the foster room, I lay down on the bed. One more time, tears began to form in my eyes, then stream down my face. I cried for myself. I cried for my mother. I cried because I had run away from my problems, my anger, my fears. I cried deeply, sobbing, choking to get enough air. Then I cried some more.

Finally, the cry was done. I felt better somehow. I got up from the bed and went to the bathroom where I washed my face at the sink. My eyes sparkled brighter. I rubbed my face dry with a yellow striped towel, just like one we had at home. I had been though so much the last year of my life. I struggled alone. And now that I had people to help me, I wasn't at all sure I could go on.

I returned to Ida Mae's room and glanced at the clock. It was nearly ten. I'd heard Ida Mae come back in the house a long time ago. She would be upstairs soon to go to bed. I changed into a pair of pajamas I had retrieved from the stash, and slipped between the cool cotton of the sheets. I intended to stay awake until Ida Mae came upstairs, but immediately I fell asleep.

***

Monday morning came quickly enough and found me washed, dressed, and fed when Ida Mae left for school. Mrs. Ruth and I weren't leaving until a quarter to nine. We had an appointment with a caseworker to discuss the things I had told Mrs. Ruth after the fire. There were lots of things Ida Mae's family didn't know about me, even though I told her about the abuse and my running away.

My caseworker was young. I liked that. She came into the room and immediately over to me. She stuck out her hand. "Good morning, Beth," she said, shaking my hand. "My name is Molly, and I'll be handling your case until we get everything resolved."

"Hi," I said. Mrs. Ruth stood next to me and I looked to her for approval.

Molly said, "I just need to start by asking you a few things."

Mrs. Ruth gave me a quick squeeze and said, "I'll be out in the front office if you need me for anything." Molly nodded her head. I was sort of surprised Ida Mae's mom left me, but it didn't seem unusual to Molly.

101

When she was gone, Molly pointed out two soft chairs and said, "Would you like to have a softer seat?"

Mrs. Ruth and I had entered the room before the caseworker and taken what felt like regulation school chairs next to the table. I nodded and took the new cushioned seat with much appreciation.

"I hate those plastic things," Molly said before sitting on one of the cushioned chairs, letting herself bounce a little to enjoy the padding. I did the same thing. "I don't know why so many government groups buy them. Probably because they're cheap."

"They have them at school," I said. "I always manage to get one that's cracked, and it pinches the back of my leg."

"Oh, yes. I remember." She laughed. Her chatter made me feel relaxed, and I realized I had been tense all morning. After so many months of hiding the truth, I wasn't sure I could once again talk easily about my situation.

"Do you like school?" Molly asked.

"Yes. I like to read, and I usually get good grades." I felt proud of those accomplishments at least, even if I did still feel guilty about running away from all my other problems.

"What sort of grades are you getting here in your classes?" Molly seemed genuinely interested.

"Mostly *A*s and *B*s. I'm even getting a good grade in choir." I'd never thought about taking choir before I left home. There hadn't been anything to sing about there anyway.

"Do you like to sing?"

"I didn't used to. But my choir teacher treats me like I already know how to sing, and tells me I'm doing a good job." I looked down, embarrassed by the next thing I wanted to say, but I said it anyway. "I feel good after her class."

A big smile crossed Molly's face. "That's important, isn't it? Feeling good about yourself?" she said, making sure I knew what she was talking about.

I nodded in agreement.

"Did you feel good about yourself before you came here?" Molly asked.

I shook my head. *No.*

"Can you tell me why?" Molly's voice was kind, but I could tell she wanted the whole truth. I'd have to give it to her.

I could feel that this was the hard stuff coming on, but I knew I had to tell her. "There was a boy living in our house who abused me."

"Was he related to you?"

"He was the son of my mom's boyfriend," I said. "His name is Ryan, and I saw him Saturday. He has been living with the Ruth family, in foster care." It was a lot for me to say all at once. But the time had come to speak up. I wanted to protect Ida Mae. I wanted to protect my mom.

And I wanted to protect me. I told Molly my story in its entirety.

Molly didn't probe too deep, just gathered a few additional facts from me. I gave my real name, Elizabeth Taylor, and my mother's address.

"Phone number?" Molly asked, her pen ready to write the numbers down.

"I'm not sure anymore." The call I'd made on Saturday hadn't gone through, but I was sure I'd dialed correctly.

Molly looked up at me, confusion on her face as she waited a second before asking, "Did you forget it?"

"No. I tried to call my mom on Saturday, and the automated operator said the phone had been disconnected. There was no other information."

"What's your mother's name?"

"Kate Taylor."

Molly scribbled Mom's name down on the paper. "Well, I'll see what we can do to help track her down. Don't worry," she said. "We'll see that your mother is found and notified you are okay."

I smiled to let her know I understood and appreciated her efforts.

"Well, that's pretty much it for me, at least right now," Molly said as she stood and prepared to leave.

"What about Ryan?" I asked, confused she hadn't asked more about him.

"Someone else will talk with you about him," she said.

"I'm just here to worry about you, and about finding your mom. I'll let you know as soon as I get any word about her," she said, as she walked to the door and left me with a little wave of her hand.

Ida Mae's mom stood up from the chair where she waited outside. "Ready for some lunch?"

I looked at the clock on the wall. It was noon already.

20

"Call me *Beth*," I said to Ida Mae, who was struggling to remember to call me by the new name—*Liz*—my old name, actually. Somehow, *Liz* didn't seem to fit me anymore, but neither did *Beth*. Both names represented someone I didn't want to be. As *Liz* I fought hard to cover up the terrible things happening to me. I had to hide the truth as *Beth*, too. I wanted my life to represent a whole new me. Suddenly, it struck me.

"No, wait," I said. "Call me Elizabeth. That's my real name. Elizabeth Taylor."

"Like the movie star?" Ida Mae asked.

"Mom named me after her on purpose. She wanted me to be just like her."

It had been nearly a week since I talked with Molly at Family Protection Services and still no word about my mother and where she might be. I wondered if she had gotten my postcard. Maybe she would have started looking for me, or maybe she would have tried to run away to protect me. Just like I had done.

I had gone back to school on Tuesday with Ida Mae, and we didn't let on anything was different about me. I still answered to *Beth* in the classroom, and the fire department kept secret the information about the shed fire being related to me—Family Protection Services likely had something to do with that. I was still living with Ida Mae and her family.

I was almost afraid to ask about Ryan, but it had already been a week, so I finally did. "He's been moved to another foster family," Mr. Ruth said. "Children aren't kept in shelter homes very long. But you don't have to worry, he won't be coming back here."

That was a relief. Despite all Ryan did to hurt me, and the fears I had about being reunited in a home with him, I never believed he knew any better about the ways he treated me. I saw the things his father did, the way he treated my mother, and I expected Ryan learned it all from watching through the years. Ryan needed help to change, but I didn't believe in hurting people out of spite. I wanted someone to help him the way Ida Mae and her parents were ready to help me.

***

I'd gotten pretty well settled this past week, school was going okay, and it was nice to be back in a real home with someone's mother to fuss over me. I'd been successful—or at least until the fire—at taking care of myself, but I'd been doing that long enough. Mr. and Mrs. Ruth were very nice to me, and they treated me like I was their own daughter, chores and all. It didn't bother me. I liked feeling needed, and I wanted to be a part of a family. I knew it would be hard to once again become a family with Mom once Molly succeeded in finding her, but I loved her, as I was sure she loved me. It would all work out okay, I was certain.

The lunch bell rang, startling me out of my reverie. I

gathered my things from my desk and headed into the crowded hallway. I stopped at my locker long enough to put my books away, then headed toward the cafeteria to look for Ida Mae and grab a bite to eat. Main line lunch was corn dogs again. I'd been eating so well at Ida Mae's, I didn't want to face a corn dog if I didn't have to. I slipped into the much shorter salad line. Ms. Meyers was entering student lunch numbers into the computer at the salad line today. We exchanged pleasantries, and I took a bowl from the sidebar and began filling it with my favorite salad things—sprouts, cheese, eggs, croutons, and sunflower seeds. At the salad bar, kids lost the need for keeping the line straight, and those behind me quickly moved ahead of me, leaving me closest to Ms. Meyers when her number-punching was done.

"Read any good books lately, Beth?"

"It's been a pretty busy week," I said. "I thought I'd start *Dicey's Song*, maybe tonight." Cynthia Voigt was one of my recently discovered favorite authors. Her stories about kids dealing with survival without the support of parents struck a familiar cord and gave me courage to go on.

"What's it about?" Ms. Meyers seemed genuinely interested.

"It's part of a series about a girl who wants to keep her family together, despite the fact their mother is gone."

"Sounds like a difficult situation to me," Ms. Meyers said.

"It can be," I almost whispered. I wasn't sure if Ms. Meyers heard me, because just then a group of kids ditched the main line and decided to join the salad line. I gave Ms. Meyers a wave good-bye and scanned the lunch room for Ida Mae. I didn't see her anywhere. I did catch a glimpse of Jill Kimball sitting with Karly Kincaide. Jill nodded my way, acknowledging me without Karly being able to see. I nodded back and moved toward an empty seat. I figured Ida Mae was running a little late and would join me any minute, so I chose a seat with an empty mate. I set the bowl and silverware on the tabletop and started to take my seat.

"You're coming with me." An all-too familiar voice. Ryan.

This couldn't be. He didn't go to this school anymore. What was he doing here? My heart started to race and the fury that welled up inside me clouded my eyes so I could hardly see. He grabbed my arm, just above the elbow in a gesture I knew well and started to walk me across the cafeteria.

"Let go of me!" Did I say it loud enough for anyone to hear?

"Not this time," he said. "You aren't getting away."

I didn't know what to do. I didn't want to go anywhere with him, especially somewhere we couldn't be seen. I resisted the direction he was taking me, angering him more.

"Cut that out!" he said, louder than either of us spoke before.

A few kids looked our way. We were almost at the door to the outside courtyard. Stopping him now was my last chance. Where were the teachers? I started to scream. "Let go of me!" I yelled over and over. I tried to pull my arm away from his grip but couldn't manage. He was too strong. "Someone call the police!" I could see no one was responding, only staring at me in total disbelief, the same way they stared at Ms. Meyers that memorable day.

I refused to let him shove me out the door. Ryan's face was filled with anger and hate, both too strongly felt to just let me go and provide his own means of escape. As I continued to struggle, I saw Jill Kimball streak past me.

"I'll call the police," she yelled as she darted through the door and across the courtyard, which led to the front office and a telephone.

Ryan had me now by both arms and was pulling me through the door. Slowly, slowly, I began to feel my hands release my own hold from the side of the door and I was being dragged. A sharp jerk from behind released me from his grip, and I staggered back, falling into the chairs and tables behind me. I looked to see who was helping me. Ms. Meyers. She lunged at Ryan, arms flailing in battle like a lioness protecting her cub. Her adult size gave her some advantage, her anger added more, and soon she had Ryan's arms taut behind his back, linked through hers in a death grip. He continued to struggle, but Ms. Meyer's arms held him fast.

"Kick boxing," I heard Ms. Meyers' say.

Just as I was starting to stand, Ida Mae came rushing through the cafeteria and caught me from behind, almost knocking me from my feet again. "Elizabeth," she said. "Are you okay?"

I stared at Ryan, an unwilling captive in the arms of Ms. Meyers. He no longer struggled.

"Yes," I said. A rush of air came from deep inside me. I knew this time I really would be okay.

"Let's go," Ms. Meyers said to Ida Mae and me as she began to direct Ryan across the courtyard in the same path Jill had taken. Ryan glared at both Ms. Meyers and Ida Mae, but he gave me a much stronger look.

"You've ruined my life," he said, then he spat toward me.

"You've ruined your own," Ms. Meyers said. She gave his arms another jerk, just to remind him who was in charge, I think.

I was glad I didn't have to speak to him.

Jill entered the front door with the campus police officer when we arrived at the front office. "That's the boy, Officer," she said, pointing toward my assailant, before running to throw her arms around me. "Are you okay? Did he hurt you?"

"Not this time," I said, noting Ida Mae's confusion at Jill's concern. A policeman took control of Ryan from Ms. Meyers, and guided him out the door, to the waiting patrol car.

"I guess you'll need to talk to me?" I asked the officer who remained.

"That would be the best thing," the officer said. Then looking around and seeing a crowd had followed us from the cafeteria, he added, "Some place private." Ms. Meyers directed us into the school's office and shut the door behind us. Ida Mae picked up the phone to call her mother as I began to sketch my personal history to the officer.

It seemed no time before Mrs. Ruth was there. Once my statements were given, I got in the car to go home with Ida Mae. The police officer took Ryan with him, and Ms. Meyers returned to the cafeteria.

21

Ida Mae and I had been awake for almost an hour, despite the fact it was Saturday. We had straightened the room and eaten breakfast and now we were lying on the bed, trying to decide what to do. Ryan had been placed at a higher security shelter until the details could be handled. I was glad I didn't have to worry about him right now.

"Elizabeth," Mrs. Ruth called to me from the bottom of the stairs. "There is someone here to see you."

"Guess that answers our question for now," Ida Mae said. "You have something to do."

"Be right down," I said to her mother. I bounced from the mattress and headed toward the stairs, unsure who the visitor might be. I figured Molly wouldn't be working on a weekend and, as far as I knew, no one had been able to locate Mom, unless the postcard really had helped her find me.

Mrs. Ruth had led the guest into the formal living room. I stepped inside. Sitting on the couch was someone I wouldn't have expected. Jill Kimball still resembled the photo. She looked uncomfortable. Just as I felt. I hadn't told Ida Mae, yet, about how Jill came to my aid at school, or even how she comforted me at the post office just a week ago. I honestly didn't know how to broach the subject without feeling like a traitor to Ida Mae. No matter what pain Jill had gone through in her own life, she had brought even more pain to Ida Mae, who was rapidly becoming the best friend I had ever had in the whole wide world.

"Hi," I said.

"I came to see how you were. I didn't see you at school yesterday." Jill played with the hem of her shirt for a minute, trying hard not to look at me.

"I spent the day at Family Protection Services," I said, although I wasn't sure why.

"That's what I figured when I saw Molly at school."

"You know Molly?" I couldn't stop myself from asking, or from still being surprised about Jill's own past.

She glanced up at me for a second. "She was my social worker."

"I see." I said, letting her sit there, working that hem almost to death. When I heard a little squeak of surprise at the entrance to the living room, I turned to look.

"Oh. I'm sorry," Ida Mae said. "I'll leave you two alone." She started to back away, a look I couldn't quite interpret on her face.

"Ida Mae," Jill said to the retreating figure. Jill jumped from her seat and ran to the doorway. "Please come back. You're the one I really came to talk to."

Ida Mae reluctantly reentered the living room, a look of confusion on her face. She took a seat on the loveseat, next to me.

Jill returned to the sofa. "Ida Mae," she said. Her voice

trembled, and she had difficulty looking Ida Mae straight in the eye. "Ida Mae, I'm . . . I've . . . I . . ." Sweat broke out on Jill's forehead as she tried to say what she came to.

"It's okay," Ida Mae said. "You don't have to . . ."

That opened the floodgates. "Oh, yes I do," Jill said, courage now allowing her to look straight at us. "Ida Mae, I've been terrible. You treated me like a sister during the time I needed to stay with you and Mr. and Mrs. Ruth. And how did I repay you? I told terrible rumors at school and made sure no one wanted you as a friend."

"They weren't rumors," Ida Mae said.

"It doesn't matter if they were true. I never should have done that to you." She stood and came over directly in front of Ida Mae, who was sitting on the seat next to me. "I came to ask if you could ever forgive me," Jill said, looking straight down at Ida Mae.

Ida Mae hesitated only slightly before she said, "Of course, I can forgive you." Jill giggled with joy as Ida Mae stood up, and the two of them flung their arms around each other. I wasn't surprised, because Ida Mae had easily forgiven me when I was unkind at first. I stood to join them and soon found myself in the middle of a hugging session like none I had ever experienced before. For the first time in a long time, I truly felt loved.

"I can't tell you how glad I am to hear you'll forgive me Ida Mae," Jill said as we resumed our seats, only this time all scrunched in on the same couch. We were chatting like lifelong friends when I heard the phone ring from the other room.

A few minutes later, Ida Mae's mother stepped into the doorway. She just beamed when she saw the three of us together, arms slung around each others' shoulders. "Elizabeth," she said. "I have some more good news."

Good news? How could anything be better than this? The three of us all under one roof, acting like sisters, and having forgiven anything that earlier came between us.

"Family services has located your mother. She had disconnected the phone, but she's okay. She will be at Molly's office on Monday afternoon." Mrs. Ruth said, her mouth was having trouble saying the words through the grin that kept popping across her face.

Now it was my turn to squeal with delight.

"She got your postcard," Mrs. Ruth said. "Soon you'll be back together."

I jumped up and ran over to her and gave her a hug. "Thank you. Oh, thank you."

"No need to thank me. We are happy to do what we can to help a sweet child like you."

My face blushed furiously at her compliment, but I didn't mind. I was here with two friends I had grown to love. Mr. and Mrs. Ruth treated me like one of their own. Ryan had gone far, far from my life. And my mother was coming to see me soon.

Life couldn't be any happier. I couldn't be any safer. At last, I felt like a member of the choir, singing a song in tune.

22

Monday morning found Ida Mae and me standing at the school bus together with Jill. Ida Mae's circle of friends certainly had grown. I was glad to see her so happy, and to see Jill so happy, too. She didn't appear as content while mistreating Ida Mae as she did now. Her friend, Karley, looked stunned when she arrived at the bus stop, a few minutes late, to see Jill, Ida Mae, and me climbing on the bus together and taking the front seat. Karley hesitated a moment, staring at Jill as if she expected an explanation. But Jill was involved in a serious conversation with Ida Mae—they found they had a lot to catch up on—and didn't even notice Karley standing in the aisle, blocking traffic.

"Go on back to a seat, Karley," Mrs. Stevens said.

Karley looked at me for a second. I flashed a wide grin and burst out laughing as I saw her stumble away. I knew we could work it all out later, once we arrived at school.

There were lots of things I could work out at school, but since the school year was winding down, I planned to leave as much of it to die over the summer as I could. I remembered how quickly the furor over Ms. Meyer's and her great run had calmed, and I figured gossip over my attack would, too, if I gave it enough time.

There was one thing I couldn't leave over the summer, though, and I knew it. I had to track down Ms. Meyers and thank her for coming to my rescue. I left Jill and Ida Mae at the school's front door, secure in our trust of each other. I would not be left out just because I wasn't with them every second of the day. I had other things to do.

I dropped off my books in my locker and headed straight for the cafeteria. With any luck, I could catch Ms. Meyers before school. I figured she'd be too busy at lunch, and I knew her shift ended before my day was through. Providence was with me. Ms. Meyers was indeed in the lunchroom. And better yet, she worked alone, straightening tables and chairs in preparation for the student windstorm due to hit at noon. She saw me coming and stopped her work to wait for me to approach.

"Hello, Ms. Meyers," I said when I caught up to her.

"How's it going, Beth?"

"Better now, thanks to you." I wanted to give her a hug, but I knew kids and adults weren't supposed to hug at school.

"No thanks necessary. I just did what I had to do." She shook the rag she was using to wipe down the tables, and a few stray pieces of yesterday's leftovers fluttered to the floor.

I brought my attention back in line and looked directly at her face. "You told me once sometimes we need rescuing. Thanks for being there."

"It's the same thing you did once for me," she said, a hint of pink rising onto her cheeks. "I'd be pretty ungrateful if I couldn't return the favor."

"Well, all the same, thank you."

"You're welcome. You'd better get going or you'll be late for class." She made a shooing motion with her hands, the rag flapping in the breeze, like she was sending a group of chickens away from the coop.

I gave my head a solid nod. "I'll see you later, then." I took off with a wave, gratitude in my heart for Ms. Meyers. I still didn't know what had happened to her, but I understood that I didn't need to know anything more than we both did what was right in a crisis.

***

Somehow I finished the last of my classes, despite my growing excitement at seeing my mother. Mrs. Ruth picked me up at school. Ida Mae rode the bus home like usual. We planned to be home around six. Mom would come with us for dinner. Both Mrs. Ruth and Molly warned me I probably would continue to stay with the Ruth family a little bit longer, while the state tried to help my mom. Mark was due to go to trial sometime this week. I had seen a small article in the paper and relished the calm feeling it gave me. As long as I knew Mom was all right, that Mark couldn't do her any more harm, I didn't mind if I stayed with Ida Mae and her family forever.

No, not really forever. I wanted to live with my own mother, but I knew she had some things to take care of herself before she was ready to live with this almost-teenage daughter. I expected I would turn thirteen before all of the pieces had been put back together. Progress. That's all I needed to make me happy.

Mom must have arrived just before we did. I recognized her stride as she crossed the parking lot before us. I started to call out, when a man rushed toward her. Mark.

My mind struggled to make sense of it. What was Mark doing here? He was supposed to be in jail, awaiting trial. Yet here he was, rushing toward my mom across the parking lot. Before I could call out a warning, he jumped her from behind. I could hear her scream as he pounded his fist against her face.

"No!" I let out a bloodcurdling cry, as I pulled loose from Mrs. Ruth and ran toward my mom. She crumpled to the ground under his weight.

"Help! Help!" I heard Mrs. Ruth cry, as I reached my mom and her assailant. I immediately started pounding my fists against his body—arms, legs, head, back—it didn't matter as long as I felt the solid contact of my skin against his muscles. He pushed me away over and over again as he continued to pound his fist against my mother's now silent body.

I was a raging machine. All the hate and anger I had ever felt came pouring out of me. I couldn't stop punching him. My blind fury kept me from knowing how much time had passed. My body was lifted away from my target.

I stopped. A police officer had me. Three police

officers threw Mark flat against the ground, snapping handcuffs around his wrists in the process. Another officer and a paramedic knelt close to my mother. Where had they come from? I couldn't remember.

The officer released me, and Mrs. Ruth was there, her strong, loving arms around me. She pulled me to her, just like the day of the fire, and said, "Everything will be all right. It's going to be okay."

My eyes were drawn to my silent and bleeding mother. A stretcher was wheeled to her motionless form, and the men gently lifted her up and strapped her to the frame. I tried to move toward her, but Mrs. Ruth held me. At first I fought her, but then my senses began to return. I knew I could be of no help as the medical people worked with Mom. Instead, I started praying. I wasn't sure anyone was listening to me, but I knew I had to try.

The medics lifted the stretcher into the back of the waiting ambulance and prepared to move her to the hospital. Just before the doors closed, I noticed a sign of life. Mom stirred. Then her voice. "Liz. Elizabeth." She whimpered. Tears streamed down my face. My mother had said my name.

"I'm here, Mom. I'm here," I said, running toward her to assure her I was fine.

The doors closed with a clang and the sirens came to life. As the ambulance pulled away, I got my first glance at Mark. His face was bruised and had been bleeding, but the paramedics had wiped most of the blood away. I could tell he was going to have a good shiner, and I was proud. It was nothing compared to the pain both he and his son had given me, but it was something. Something tangible, that at least he could see for a time. Maybe it would be enough to remind him of me.

23

Mom spent the next several days in at special unit at the hospital, recovering once again from the wounds she received from her boyfriend. All the time she was there, counselors worked with her, helping her overcome some of the emotional trauma as well. I worked with counselors, too. Slowly I began to see that we both were getting better.

I stayed on with Ida Mae's family. I expected to for a while, giving Mom plenty of time to recuperate and put her life back together. "Once I get a new job, things will be better," She promised, and I believed her. I knew Mom and I could make it together. We didn't need Mark. We didn't need my dad, either. I figured it was time I forget about him altogether.

We did need the help of the counselors and social workers like Molly. They were there to help us put back the pieces. And, the Ruth family—Mr. Ruth, Mrs. Ruth, and Ida Mae—along with Ms. Meyers and Jill Kimball. We needed them too.

Mark had been sent to prison for attempted murder. Ida Mae's mom had been called to testify, the same as I was. We went to the courthouse, and I told the story of the last few years, including the events which had happened the day in the parking lot. Mrs. Ruth corroborated my story, adding details only she had seen while I had attacked Mark.

Two of the officers who had responded were also called to the stand, verifying details and giving the prosecution even more credence. The jury gave a unanimous *Guilty.*

A few days later, Mrs. Ruth and I testified at a second court, one exclusively for juveniles. Again I told the story of the abuse by Ryan and the attack in the cafeteria. Ms. Meyers came to tell her side of the story, as well. The three of us together were all it took to paint the picture of the horrors of my life. My mother was excused from the proceedings of both cases because her doctors wouldn't release her from the hospital yet. Mark had beaten her much more severely this time, despite my efforts to intervene. Her release wasn't necessary as Ryan's decision came back the same as his father's: *Guilty.* The only difference was Ryan would not go to prison like his father. He would be entered into a counseling program at a group home.

Life was back on an even keel. I had my mom back and she would eventually be okay. I had the greatest new family. And my friends were first rate. For the first time in my life, my grades were straight *A*s. Who could ask for a better life? Not me.

***

Mom was sitting on the Ruths' couch and looking better than I'd seen her in some time. The rosy color was back in her cheeks and a sparkle in her eyes. She'd managed to put on a little weight and the bruises had faded.

"What do you want to do now that that part of our life is over, Lizzy?"

"Elizabeth," I said.

"Elizabeth," she said.

Good, she recognized I was a new me. "I want you to get better," I said. "And, if it's okay with you, I'd like to stay here with my new life. You could get a job here, couldn't you?"

"I think it could be arranged," she said. "I really like your new friends."

"Yeah, they're great, especially Ida Mae."

"Especially Ida Mae's mother," Mom said. "I think she's going to be the one to save me."

"I hope not," I said. I'd already learned the truth for myself, but Mom didn't need to run away like I had to figure it out.

"Why not?" she asked, her confusion written all over her face.

"You have to save yourself," I said.

"But sometimes you need someone to rescue you," Mom said. "Elizabeth Taylor always said . . ."

Thinking of the day I ran away, I started to protest. "No more Elizabeth Taylor stories, Mom."

Without warning, a flash of history ran through my mind. Ms. Meyers running like crazy past the bus and me tearing close behind. My standing up for Ida Mae at the bus stop when Jill and the small children teased her about the

126

wet bed. Jill Kimball sitting beside me on the post office steps. Mrs. Ruth cuddling me in the lawn after the fire. And all the events leading up to where people rushed into my life to help me and my mother survive.

I heard once again the wisdom of Ms. Meyers. I knew she was right. I needed people to rescue me. And so did my mother. Ida Mae's family gave us the support system we needed right now.

And we would make it again on our own.

Someday.

24

"Hey, Mom!" I called, as I entered the apartment, my arms loaded down with new books from the library. I pushed the door shut with the back of my foot and headed down the hallway to my bedroom. "I'm home." *Home.* What an incredible word it had come to be.

"Elizabeth, where are you?" I heard my mom call from the kitchen.

"In my bedroom. I'll be right there," I said, as I dumped the books onto my bed. My own bed in my own room. What a glorious place.

"Come out into the kitchen, Honey," Mom said. "I need your help."

I straightened my shirt into place, disheveled by the weight of the books, and headed down the hallway, through the living room and into the kitchen.

"Surprise!" Everyone was there—my mother, Ida Mae, Jill Kimball, Mr. and Mrs. Ruth, Ms. Meyers, even Molly, my former social worker.

"What's this?" I asked, taken aback at the gathering.

"Happy Birthday!" they said in unison.

"Happy Birthday? But my birthday was three weeks ago."

"True," my mother stepped forward to say. "But we were so busy with the moving and getting settled I couldn't surprise you then."

Lu Ann Brobst Staheli

"I didn't need a party. Just having you back was a great enough birthday for me." I gave her a hug. "Thanks, everyone."

It's not every day a girl becomes a teenager," Ida Mae's mom said.

"Welcome to the club," Jill said, coming over to give Elizabeth a hug of her own.

And Ida Mae said, "I expect you at my party." She grabbed them both in a group hug.

"You can count on it," I said with a wink toward Ida Mae's mother.

Mom approached the table, carrying a chocolate cake. "Make a wish and blow out the candles."

I closed my eyes and said my secret wish—my friendships and loves would go on just like today for the rest of my life. I sucked in a big breath and let it all out, snuffing each candle in its wake. Tears welled in my eyes as I looked around at my complete family. And I knew my wish would come true. And I *would* continue to survive.

Just like Elizabeth Taylor.

Recommended Reading

For more information about the real Elizabeth Taylor, check your local library or favorite online sources. These are the books I read from my local library at the time this book was drafted:

Guiliano, Geoffrey. *Elizabeth Taylor: A Tribute*. New York: Random House, 1999.

Kelly, Kitty. *Elizabeth Taylor: The Last Star*. New York: Simon & Shuster, 1981

Sheppard, Dick. Elizabeth: *The Life and Times of Elizabeth Taylor*. New York: Warner Books, 1976.

Taraborrello, J. Randy. *Elizabeth.* New York: Warner Books, 2006.

Acknowledgements

Since my childhood, whenever people asked me what I wanted to be when I grew up, I said I wanted to be an author. But I lived in a small town in Indiana where I knew nothing about how to get published, nor did I know anyone who did, expect for those who were writing for the local newspaper. At the time, I thought newspaper writing was not for me. I wanted to write novels, but I didn't know what I would do with a manuscript once I got it written.

Fast forward several years when my heart told me it was time to move to Utah. Within a few months of living here, I had learned about the League of Utah Writers and signed up to attend the conference they were soon having. I don't remember who gave the keynote that year, but I do remember all the things I learned about publishing, query letters, and submissions. Suddenly I felt like all my questions had been answered, although I soon found there was much more to learn, so I became a member of LUW, attended monthly meetings, made lots of knowledgeable friends, and started writing more seriously.

All that I learned in my years with the LUW has guided me toward the publication history I have today. I'd like to thank those I met there who helped me get my start: Brenda Bensch, who has always been one of my biggest supporters; Rick Walton, whose impressive career serves as an inspiration; and Stephanni Hicken Meyer, who came to me with the idea to start our own critique group.

We've gone through many changes in membership since those early days, but my critique group is definitely one of the best in the world: Annette Lyon, Michele Paige Holmes, J. Scott Savage, Heather B. Moore, Robison Wells, and Sarah M. Eden.

I'd also like to thank Joan Bauer, John H. Ritter, Tim Wynn-Jones, and my friend and author extraordinaire, Carol Lynch Williams, for their valuable input on the opening chapters.

Thanks to Jaimey Grant for putting up with the numerous emails as we finalized the cover design. She has an incredible talent for picking just the right look for each book, yet keeping the integrity of the series intact.

And Lisa Harrison, I'm glad you came into my library often enough that we became great friends. I'll miss you there next year, but you know you'll hear from me often anyway.

Of course, none of this would be possible without the support of my husband, Mike, and our sons: Carl, Tommy, Chan, Kent, and Zach.

About the Author

Lu Ann Brobst Staheli got her start as a celebrity paparazzi-stalker-chick, which led to her award-winning career as a ghostwriter for celebrity memoirs. A masochist at heart, she taught junior high school English for 33 years, moved to the school library beginning year 34, and once spent two weeks summer vacation backpacking through Europe with fifteen of her students. She has won three Best of State Medals—two for writing and one for teaching—but refuses to wear them all at the same time because she'd hate to be known as a show-off. Her other published works include *The Explorers: Tides Across the Sea; Leona & Me, Helen Marie; A Note With Taking; When Hearts Conjoin,*

the story of the conjoined Herrin twins; *Psychic Madman* about mentalist Jim Karol; *One Day at a Time: Teaching Secondary Language Arts*; and *Books, Books, and More Books: A Parent and Teacher's Guide to Adolescent Literature*. Lu Ann says, "But 2013 will be the year of the eBook for me. A long list of titles are in the finalization stage, and I'm excited to make them available to my readers."

Lu Ann's articles have appeared in Grit, Byline, Scouting, Library Media Connections, and The Writer magazines, and she is featured in the upcoming book release, *Best of The Writer*. She has published invitational essays in *Teaching Secondary Language Arts K-12: It Really Works* (Christopher-Gordon Publishers) and *Famous Family Nights* (Cedar Fort International).

As a Senior Editor with Precision Editing Group, Lu Ann Staheli has had a hand in a number of releases from Deseret Book, Shadow Mountain, Covenant Communications, and other regional publishers, including several winners and finalists for the Whitney Award and New York Times bestsellers. A former Associate Producer of Alan Osmond's Stadium of Fire, Lu Ann resides in Spanish Fork, Utah, with her husband, and tries to keep track of their five sons.

The Small Town U.S.A. Series

A Note Worth Taking

The end of eighth grade should be an exciting and happy time for Laura Breathnach. But when her best friend gives her a note saying their friendship is over, Laura can't figure out what hit her. Still reeling, Laura goes to science class only to find out she needs a partner for the school science fair. Vickie, who has always been her project partner before now, chooses a popular girl who hangs out with Laura's worst enemy. Laura realizes she can only get over the loss of an old friend by making new ones. When Kim asks Laura to be her partner, she accepts. In addition, Laura spends more time with a band buddy who shares her love of music. Even as Laura tries to heal from the pain of lost friendship, she keeps an eye on Vickie and her new friends, hoping to see a turn in the tide of popularity, and wondering if a friendship is really one worth saving.

"This story should be a must-read for every middle grade/junior high girl. The hurt that Laura, the main character, suffers at the hand of Vickie, her supposed best friend, is one that so many girls this age will relate to. How Laura handles the school situation and her pain, along with the growth she experiences throughout the story, are what make this book stand out. Good lessons and good times. Adults reading the story will enjoy the nostalgia of days gone by—as well as being grateful those days are past. We all survived junior high! Laura does too, and you'll cheer for her triumphs over mean girls and her blossoming maturity and self-worth."

—Michele Paige Homes, Whitney Award-winning author

Leona & Me, Helen Marie

Seven-year-old Helen Marie Heffner has a knack for getting into trouble, followed close behind by her older sister, Leona Mae. Whether it's walking the barn beams like a tightrope, fooling the neighbor boys into thinking they're being chased by a fiery jack-o-lantern, or making a mess rather than transferring a pattern for Mama's Christmas surprise, Helen comes out the winner every time. But life is not always fun and games in 1922 for this southern Indiana family. In the wake of the Depression of the previous two years, the girls and their mama are often left alone in Hancock's Chapel while their papa travels to find work to keep the family finances alive. Lately, Mama's been showing signs of not feeling well, and Helen is stuck at home, missing the entire school year while she recuperates from the rheumatic fever that struck her the year before. Mama fears the worst is about to happen. Everything from the barn owl, to the chicken thief, the stranger who passed by one evening to a poor neighbor-boy who falls into the ravine, all point to signs of trouble to come. And sure enough, it does.

"A delightful middle grade novel from award-winning author, Lu Ann Staheli. Readers will fall in love with Helen Marie, a precocious seven-year-old, who looks up to her older sister, Leona Mae, the two of them getting into trouble more often or not (think Laura Ingalls . . .). I laughed out loud at Helen Marie's antics and loved her relationship with her mother and father. Set in 1922 southern Indiana, the family faces financial hardships, like so many around them. But they are blessed with a humble life, rich with country living, and take pride in hard work."

—H. B. Moore, Utah Best of State and Whitney Award-winning author

The Explorers Series

Tides Across the Sea

Set against the background of the exploration of the Aztec civilization, *Tides Across the Sea*, opens in the year 1519, where the passion for adventure and the lust for gold reign in the hearts of both young and old. Fifteen-year-old Felipe is no exception, though his yearning for adventure is tempered by his love for the beautiful Manuela. She wants to marry Felipe, but she must first rid herself of the betrothal bands her papa has accepted on her behalf to the local bully, who threatens the life of the one she loves. When Felipe ends up on Cortés' ship bound for the New World, the young couple is pulled apart.

Felipe and Manuela each must find a way to overcome the odds stacked against them if they want to someday reunite. But the New World is filled with danger, and Felipe may not escape the human sacrifices being made to the Great White God, unless the young slave girl, Tia, who also yearns for home, can help him escape and return to Manuela.

"A good read for the 12–16 age range and is a beautiful coming of age and young love story. The author obviously did an extensive amount of research and it shows in the scenery, language and tone of the book. There is plenty of action, following not only the main couple, but also a young slave girl in the palace of Montezuma. Both sides continue to build until the truth of Cortez's expedition comes to a head . . . *Tides Across the Sea* sends young readers deep into history and gives them a story they will find difficult to put down!"
—Stephenia McGeen, InD'Tale Magazine

www.ingramcontent.com/pod-product-compliance
Lightning Source LLC
Chambersburg PA
CBHW070335130626
46556CB00007B/2880